PRAISE FOR
THE WAY HOME

"With beautiful world-building and tons of heart, these tender fantasies are sure to delight."
—*Publishers Weekly* (starred review)

"The writing in 'Sooz' is particularly lush and lyrical, with beautiful and desolate descriptions of the world of the Dreamies and the simultaneously magical and terrible things that happen there." —Paste

"Beagle brilliantly balances the bits of darkness that exist with Sooz's drive to accomplish whatever needs to be done." —*Booklist*

"A lovely duology that invokes the charm of *The Last Unicorn* while extending the magic of the original into a bigger world. Highly recommended for lovers of Beagle's classic, who are legion." —*Library Journal*

Beagle's prose . . . is as crystalline as ever, and Sooz's voice is at once a convincing evocation of adolescent search for identity, an insightful exploration of how friendships are made, and a sense of otherworldly wonder as genuine as that of *The Last Unicorn*." —*Locus*

PRAISE FOR PETER S. BEAGLE

"One of my favorite writers."
—Madeleine L'Engle, author of *A Wrinkle in Time*

"Peter S. Beagle illuminates with his own particular magic such commonplace matters as ghosts, unicorns, and werewolves. For years a loving readership has consulted him as an expert on those hearts' reasons that reason does not know."
—Ursula K. Le Guin, author of *A Wizard of Earthsea*

"Peter S. Beagle is (in no particular order) a wonderful writer, a fine human being, and a bandit prince out to steal readers' hearts."
—Tad Williams, author of *The Dragonbone Chair*

"Peter Beagle deserves a seat at the table with the great masters of fantasy."
—Christopher Moore, author of *Lamb*

"Peter S. Beagle has both opulence of imagination and mastery of style."
—*New York Times Book Review*

"Everything Beagle writes is a pleasure to read."
—*Denver Post*

WORKS BY PETER S. BEAGLE

NOVELS

A Fine and Private Place

The Last Unicorn

Lila the Werewolf

The Folk of the Air

The Innkeeper's Song

The Unicorn Sonata

Tamsin

A Dance for Emilia

Return

Summerlong

In Calabria

The Last Unicorn: The Lost Journey

NONFICTION

I See by My Outfit

The California Feeling
(with Michael Bry)

American Denim

The Lady and Her Tiger
(with Pat Derby)

The Garden of Earthly Delights

In the Presence of Elephants
(with Pat Derby)

THE
WAY HOME

TWO NOVELLAS FROM THE WORLD
OF *THE LAST UNICORN*

PETER S. BEAGLE

ACE
NEW YORK

ACE
Published by Berkley
An imprint of Penguin Random House LLC
penguinrandomhouse.com

ACE is a registered trademark and the A colophon is a trademark of
Penguin Random House LLC.

"Two Hearts" first appeared in *The Magazine of Fantasy & Science Fiction*,
October/November 2005.

ISBN: 9780593547403

The Library of Congress has cataloged the Ace hardcover edition of this book as follows:

Names: Beagle, Peter S., author. | Beagle, Peter S. Two hearts. | Beagle, Peter S. Sooz.
Title: The way home : two novellas from the world of The last unicorn / Peter S. Beagle.
Description: New York : Ace, [2023]
Identifiers: LCCN 2022043477 (print) | LCCN 2022043478 (ebook) |
ISBN 9780593547397 (hardcover) | ISBN 9780593547410 (ebook)
Subjects: LCGFT: Fantasy fiction. | Novellas.
Classification: LCC PS3552.E13 W39 2023 (print) | LCC PS3552.E13 (ebook) |
DDC 813/.54—dc23/eng/20221024
LC record available at https://lccn.loc.gov/2022043477
LC ebook record available at https://lccn.loc.gov/2022043478

Ace hardcover edition / April 2023
Ace trade paperback edition / March 2024

Printed in the United States of America
1st Printing

Book design by Daniel Brount

TWO HEARTS

MY BROTHER, WILFRID, KEEPS SAYING IT'S not fair that it should all have happened to me. Me being a girl, and a baby, and too stupid to lace up my own sandals properly. But *I* think it's fair. I think everything happened exactly the way it should have done. Except for the sad parts, and maybe those, too.

I'm Sooz, and I am nine years old. Ten next month, on the anniversary of the day the griffin came. Wilfrid says it was because of me, that the griffin heard that the ugliest baby in the world had just been born, and it was going to eat me, but I was *too* ugly, even for a griffin. So it nested in the Midwood (we call it that, but its real name is the Midnight Wood, because of the darkness under the trees),

3

and stayed to eat our sheep and our goats. Griffins do that if they like a place.

But it didn't ever eat children, not until this year.

I only saw it once—I mean, once *before*—rising up above the trees one night, like a second moon. Only there wasn't a moon, then. There was nothing in the whole world but the griffin, golden feathers all blazing on its lion's body and eagle's wings, with its great front claws like teeth, and that monstrous beak that looked so huge for its head. Wilfrid says I screamed for three days, but he's lying, and I *didn't* hide in the root cellar like he says, either, I slept in the barn those two nights, with our dog Malka. Because I knew Malka wouldn't let anything get me.

I mean my parents wouldn't have, either, not if they could have stopped it. It's just that Malka is the biggest, fiercest dog in the whole village, and she's not afraid of anything. And after the griffin took Jehane, the blacksmith's little girl, you couldn't help seeing how frightened my father was, running back and forth with the other men, trying to organize some sort of patrol, so people could always tell when the griffin was coming. I know he was frightened for me and my mother, and doing everything he could to protect us, but it didn't make me feel any safer, and Malka did.

But nobody knew what to do, anyway. Not my father, nobody. It was bad enough when the griffin was only taking the sheep, because almost everyone here sells wool or cheese or sheepskin things to make a living. But once it took Jehane, early last spring, that changed everything. We sent messengers to the king—three of them—and each time the king sent someone back to us with them. The first time, it was one knight, all by himself. His name was Douros, and he gave me an apple. He rode away into the Midwood, singing, to look for the griffin, and we never saw him again.

The second time—after the griffin took Louli, the boy who worked for the miller—the king sent five knights together. One of them did come back, but he died before he could tell anyone what happened.

The third time an entire squadron came. That's what my father said, anyway. I don't know how many soldiers there are in a squadron, but it was a lot; and they were all over the village for two days, pitching their tents everywhere, stabling their horses in every barn, and boasting in the tavern how they'd soon take care of that griffin for us poor peasants. They had musicians playing when they marched into the Midwood—I remember that, and I remember when the music stopped, and the sounds we heard afterward.

After that, the village didn't send to the king anymore. We didn't want more of his men to die, and besides they weren't any help. So from then on all the children were hurried indoors when the sun went down and the griffin woke from its day's rest to hunt again. We couldn't play together or run errands or watch the flocks for our parents or even sleep near open windows, for fear of the griffin. There was nothing for me to do but read books I already knew by heart and complain to my mother and father, who were too tired from watching after Wilfrid and me to bother with us. They were guarding the other children, too, turn and turn about with the other families—*and* our sheep, *and* our goats—so they were always tired, as well as frightened; and we were all angry with each other most of the time. It was the same for everybody.

And then the griffin took Felicitas.

Felicitas couldn't talk, but she was my best friend, always, since we were little. I always understood what she wanted to say, and she understood me, better than anyone, and we played in a special way that I won't ever play with anyone else. Her family thought she was a waste of food, because no boy would marry a dumb girl, so they let her eat with us most of the time.

Wilfrid used to make fun of the whispery quack that was the one sound she could make, but I hit him with a rock, and after that he didn't do it anymore.

I didn't see it happen, but I still see it in my head. She *knew* not to go out, but she was always just so happy coming to us in the evening. And nobody at her house would have noticed her being gone. None of them ever noticed Felicitas.

The day I learned Felicitas was gone, that was the day I set off to see the king myself.

Well, the same *night*, actually—because there wasn't any chance of getting away from my house or the village in daylight. I don't know what I'd have done, really, except that my uncle Ambrose was carting a load of sheepskins to market in Hagsgate, and you have to start long before sunup to be there by the time the market opens. Uncle Ambrose is my best uncle, but I knew I couldn't ask him to take me to the king—he'd have gone straight to my mother instead, and told her to give me sulphur and molasses and put me to bed with a mustard plaster. He gives his *horse* sulphur and molasses, even.

So I went to bed early that night, and I waited until everyone was asleep. I wanted to leave a note on my pillow, but I kept writing things and then tearing the notes up and throwing them in the fireplace, and I was afraid of somebody waking or Uncle Ambrose leaving without me. Finally I just wrote, *I will come home soon.* I didn't take any clothes with me, or anything else, except a bit of cheese, because I thought the king must live somewhere near Hagsgate, which is the only big town I've ever seen. My mother and father were snoring in their room, but Wilfrid had fallen asleep right in front of the hearth, and they always leave him there when he does. If you rouse him to go to his own bed, he comes up fighting and crying. I don't know why.

I stood and looked down at him for the longest time. Wilfrid doesn't look nearly so mean when he's sleeping. My mother had banked the coals to make sure there'd be a fire for tomorrow's bread, and my father's moleskin trews were hanging there to dry, because he'd had to wade into the stock pond that afternoon to rescue a lamb. I moved them a little bit, so they wouldn't burn. I wound the clock—Wilfrid's supposed to do that every night, but he always forgets—and I thought how they'd all be hearing it ticking in the morning while they were looking everywhere for me, too frightened to eat any breakfast, and I turned to go back to my room.

But then I turned around again, and I climbed out of the kitchen window, because our front door squeaks so. I was afraid that Malka might wake in the barn and right away know I was up to something, because I can't ever fool Malka, only she didn't; and then I held my breath almost the whole way as I ran to Uncle Ambrose's house and scrambled right into his cart with the sheepskins. It was a cold night, but under that pile of sheepskins it was hot and nasty smelling; and there wasn't anything to do but lie still and wait for Uncle Ambrose. So I mostly thought about Felicitas, to keep from feeling so bad about leaving home and everyone. That was bad enough—I never really *lost* anybody close before, not *forever*—but anyway it was different.

I don't know when Uncle Ambrose finally came,

because I dozed off in the cart, and didn't wake until there was this jolt and a rattle and the sort of floppy grumble a horse makes when *he's* been waked up and doesn't like it—and we were off for Hagsgate. The moon was setting early, but I could see the village bumping by, not looking silvery in the light, but small and dull, no color to anything. And all the same I almost began to cry, because it already seemed so far away, though we hadn't even passed the stock pond yet, and I felt as though I'd never see it again. I would have climbed back out of the cart right then, if I hadn't known better.

Because the griffin was still up and hunting. I couldn't see it, of course, under the sheepskins (and I had my eyes shut, anyway), but its wings made a sound like a lot of knives being sharpened all together, and sometimes it gave a cry that was dreadful because it was so soft and gentle, and even a little sad and *scared*, as though it were imitating the sound Felicitas might have made when it took her. I burrowed deep down as I could, and tried to sleep again, but I couldn't.

Which was just as well, because I didn't want to ride all the way into Hagsgate, where Uncle Ambrose was bound to find me when he unloaded his sheepskins in the marketplace. So when I didn't hear the griffin anymore (they won't hunt far from their nests, if they don't have to), I put my head out over the tailboard of the cart and watched the stars going out, one by one, as the sky grew lighter. The dawn breeze came up as the moon went down.

When the cart stopped jouncing and shaking so much, I knew we must have turned onto the King's Highway, and when I could hear cows munching and talking softly to each other, I dropped into the road. I stood there for a little, brushing off lint and wool bits, and watching Uncle Ambrose's cart rolling on away from me. I hadn't ever been this far from home by myself. Or so lonely. The breeze brushed dry grass against my ankles, and I didn't have any idea which way to go.

I didn't even know the king's name—I'd never heard anyone call him anything but *the king*. I knew he didn't live in Hagsgate, but in a big castle somewhere nearby, only nearby's one thing when you're riding in a cart and different when you're walking. And I kept thinking about my family waking up and looking for me, and the cows' grazing sounds made me hungry, and I'd eaten all my cheese in the cart. I wished I had a penny with me—not to buy anything with, but only to toss up and let it tell me if I should turn left or right. I tried it with flat stones, but I never could find them after they came down. Finally I started off going left, not for any reason, but only because I have a little silver ring on my left hand that my mother gave me. There was a sort of path that way, too, and I thought maybe I could walk around Hagsgate and then I'd think about what to do after that. I'm a good walker. I can walk anywhere, if you give me time.

Only it's easier on a real road. The path gave out after a while, and I had to push my way through trees growing too close together, and then through so many brambly vines that my hair was full of stickers and my arms were all stinging and bleeding. I was tired and sweating, and almost crying—*almost*—and whenever I sat down to rest, bugs and things kept crawling over me. Then I heard running water nearby, and that made me thirsty right away, so I tried to get down to the sound. I had to crawl most of the way, scratching my knees and elbows up something awful.

It wasn't much of a stream—in some places the water came up barely above my ankles—but I was so glad to see it I practically hugged and kissed it, flopping down with my face buried in it, the way I do with Malka's smelly old fur. And I drank until I couldn't hold any more, and then I sat on a stone and let the tiny fish tickle my nice cold feet, and felt the sun on my shoulders, and I didn't think about griffins or kings or my family or anything.

I only looked up when I heard the horses whickering a little way upstream. They were playing with the water, the way horses do, blowing bubbles like children. Plain old livery-stable horses, one brownish, one grayish. The gray's rider was out of the saddle, peering at the horse's left forefoot. I couldn't get a good look—they both had on plain cloaks, dark green, and trews so worn you couldn't make out the color—so I didn't know that one was a woman until I heard her voice. A nice voice, low, like Silky Joan, the lady my mother won't ever let me ask about, but with something rough in it, too, as though she could scream like a hawk if she wanted to. She was saying, "There's no stone I can see. Maybe a thorn?"

The other rider, the one on the brown horse, answered her, "Or a bruise. Let me see."

That voice was lighter and younger sounding than the woman's voice, but I already knew he was a man, because he was so tall. He got down off the brown horse and the woman moved aside to let him pick up her horse's hoof. Before he did that, he put his hands on the horse's head, one on each side, and he said something to it that I couldn't quite hear. *And the horse said something back.* Not like a neigh, or a whinny, or any of the sounds horses make, but like one person talking to another. I can't say it any better than that. The tall man bent down then, and he took hold of the hoof and looked at it for a long time, and the horse didn't move or switch its tail or anything.

"A stone splinter," the man said after a while. "It's very small, but it's worked itself deep into the hoof, and there's an ulcer brewing. I can't think why I didn't notice it straightaway."

"Well," the woman said. She touched his shoulder. "You can't notice everything."

The tall man seemed angry with himself, the way my father gets when he's forgotten to close the pasture gate properly, and our neighbor's black ram gets in and fights with our poor old Brimstone. He said, "I can. I'm supposed to." Then he turned his back to the horse and bent over that forefoot, the way our blacksmith does, and he went to work on it.

I couldn't see what he was doing, not exactly. He didn't have any picks or pries, like the blacksmith, and all I'm sure of is that I *think* he was singing to the horse. But I'm not sure it was proper singing. It sounded more like the little made-up rhymes that really small children chant to themselves when they're playing in the dirt, all alone. No tune, just up and down, *dee-dah*, *dee-dah*, *dee* . . . boring even for a horse, I'd have thought. He kept doing it for a long time, still bending with that hoof in his hand. All at once he stopped singing and stood up, holding something that glinted in the sun the way the stream did, and he showed it to the horse, first thing. "There," he said, "there, that's what it was. It's all right now."

He tossed the thing away and picked up the hoof again, not singing, only touching it very lightly with one finger, brushing across it again and again. Then he set the hoof down, and the horse stamped once, hard, and whinnied, and the tall man turned to the woman and said, "We ought to camp here for the night, all the same. They're both weary, and my back hurts."

The woman laughed. A deep, sweet, slow sound, it was. I'd never heard a laugh like that.

She said, "The greatest wizard walking the world, and your back hurts? Heal it as you healed mine, the time the tree fell on me. That took you all of five minutes, I believe."

"Longer than that," the man answered her. "You were delirious, you wouldn't remember." He touched her hair, which was thick and pretty, even though it was mostly gray. "You know how I am about that," he said. "I still like being mortal too much to use magic on myself. It spoils it somehow—it dulls the feeling. I've told you before."

The woman said, "*Mmphh*," the way I've heard my mother say it a thousand times. "Well, *I've* been mortal all my life, and some days. . . ."

She didn't finish what she was saying, and the tall man smiled, the way you could tell he was teasing her. "Some days, what?"

"Nothing," the woman said, "nothing, nothing." She sounded irritable for a moment, but she put her hands on the man's arms, and she said in a different voice, "Some days—some early mornings—when the wind smells of blossoms I'll never see, and there are fawns playing in the misty orchards, and you're yawning and mumbling and scratching your head, and growling that we'll see rain before nightfall, and probably hail as well, on such mornings I wish with all my heart that we could both live forever, and I think you were a great fool to give it up." She laughed again, but it sounded shaky now, a little. She said, "Then I remember things I'd rather not remember, so then my stomach acts up, and all sorts of other things start *twinging* me—never mind what they are or where they hurt, whether it's my body or my head, or my heart. And then I think, *No, I suppose not, maybe not*." The tall man put his arms around her, and for a moment she rested her head on his chest. I couldn't hear what she said after that.

I didn't think I'd made any noise, but the man raised his voice a little, not looking at me, not lifting his head, and he said, "Child, there's food here." First I couldn't move, I was so frightened. He *couldn't* have seen me through the brush and all the alder trees. And then I started remembering how hungry I was, and I started toward them without knowing I was doing it. I actually looked down at my feet and watched them moving like somebody else's feet, as though they were the hungry ones, only they had to have me take them to the food. The man and the woman stood very still and waited for me.

Close to, the woman looked younger than her voice, and the tall man looked older. No, that isn't it, that's not what I mean. She wasn't young at all, but the gray hair made her face younger, and she held herself really straight, like the lady who comes when women in our village are having babies. She holds her face all stiff, too, that one, and I don't like her much. This woman's face wasn't beautiful, I suppose, but it was a face you'd want to snuggle up to on a cold night. That's the best I know how to say it.

The man . . . one minute he looked younger than my father, and the next he'd be looking older than anybody I ever saw, older than people are supposed to *be*, maybe. He didn't have any gray hair himself, but he did have a lot of lines, but that's not what I'm talking about, either. It was the eyes. His eyes were green, green, *green*, not like grass, not like emeralds—I saw an emerald once, a gypsy woman showed me—and not anything like apples or limes or such stuff. Maybe like the ocean, except I've never seen the ocean, so I don't know. If you go deep enough into the woods (not the Midwood, of course not, but any other sort of woods), sooner or later you'll always come to a place where even the *shadows* are green, and that's the way his eyes were. I was afraid of his eyes at first.

The woman gave me a peach and watched me bite into it, too hungry to thank her. She asked me, "Girl, what are you doing here? Are you lost?"

"No, I'm not," I mumbled with my mouth full. "I just don't know where I am—that's different." They both laughed, but it wasn't a mean, making-fun laugh. I told them, "My name's Sooz, and I have to see the king. He lives somewhere right nearby, doesn't he?"

They looked at each other. I couldn't tell what they were thinking, but the tall man raised his eyebrows, and the woman shook her head a bit, slowly. They looked at each other for a long time, until the woman said, "Well, not nearby, but not so very far, either. We were bound on our way to visit him ourselves."

"Good," I said. "Oh, *good*." I was trying to sound as grown-up as they were, but it was hard, because I was so happy to find out that they could take me to the king. I said, "I'll go along with you, then."

The woman was against it before I got the first words out. She said to the tall man, "No, we couldn't. We don't know how things are." She looked sad about it, but she looked firm, too. She said, "Girl, it's not you worries me. The king is a good man, and an old friend, but it has been a long time, and kings change. Even more than other people, kings change."

"I have to see him," I said. "You go on, then. I'm not going home until I see him." I finished the peach, and the man handed me a chunk of dried fish and smiled at the woman as I tore into it. He said quietly to her, "It seems to me that you and I both remember asking to be taken along on a quest. I can't speak for you, but I begged."

But the woman wouldn't let up. "We could be bringing her into great peril. You can't take the chance, it isn't right!"

He began to answer her, but I interrupted—my mother would have slapped me halfway across the kitchen. I shouted at them, "I'm *coming* from great peril. There's a griffin nested in the Midwood, and he's eaten Jehane and Louli and—and my Felicitas—" and then I *did* start weeping, and I didn't care. I just stood there and shook and wailed, and dropped the dried fish. I tried to pick it up, still crying so hard I couldn't see it, but the woman stopped me and gave me her scarf to dry my eyes and blow my nose. It smelled nice.

"Child," the tall man kept saying, "child, don't take on so, we didn't know about the griffin." The woman was holding me against her side, smoothing my hair and glaring at him as though it was his fault that I was howling like that. She said, "Of course we'll take you with us, girl dear— there, never mind, of course we will. That's a fearful matter, a griffin, but the king will know what to do about it. The king eats griffins for breakfast snacks—spreads them on toast with orange marmalade and gobbles them up, I promise you." And so on, being silly, but making me feel better, while the man went on pleading with me not to cry. I finally stopped when he pulled a big red handkerchief out of his pocket, twisted and knotted it into a bird shape, and made it fly away. Uncle Ambrose does tricks with coins and shells, but he can't do anything like that.

His name was Schmendrick, which I still think is the funniest name I've heard in my life.

The woman's name was Molly Grue. We didn't leave right away, because of the horses, but made camp where we were instead. I was waiting for the man, Schmendrick, to do it by magic, but he only built a fire, set out their blankets, and drew water from the stream like anyone else, while she hobbled the horses and put them to graze. I gathered firewood.

The woman, Molly, told me that the king's name was Lír, and that they had known him when he was a very young man, before he became king. "He is a true hero," she said, "a dragon slayer, a giant killer, a rescuer of maidens, a solver of impossible riddles. He may be the greatest hero of all, because he's a good man as well. They aren't always."

"But you didn't want me to meet him," I said. "Why was that?"

Molly sighed. We were sitting under a tree, watching the sun go down, and she was brushing things out of my hair. She said, "He's old now. Schmendrick has trouble with time—I'll tell you why one day, it's a long story— and he doesn't understand that Lír may no longer be the man he was. It could be a sad reunion." She started braiding my hair around my head, so it wouldn't get in the way. "I've had an unhappy feeling about this journey from the beginning, Sooz. But *he* took a notion that Lír needed us, so here we are. You can't argue with him when he gets like that."

"A good wife isn't supposed to argue with her husband," I said. "My mother says you wait until he goes out, or he's asleep, and then you do what you want."

Molly laughed, that rich, funny sound of hers, like a kind of deep gurgle. "Sooz, I've only known you a few hours, but I'd bet every penny I've got right now—aye, and all of Schmendrick's, too—that you'll be arguing on your wedding night with whomever you marry.

"Anyway, Schmendrick and I aren't married. We're together, that's all. We've been together quite a long while."

"Oh," I said. I didn't know any people who were together like that, not the way she said it. "Well, you *look* married. You sort of do."

Molly's face didn't change, but she put an arm around my shoulders and hugged me close for a moment. She whispered in my ear, "I wouldn't marry him if he were the last man in the world. He eats wild radishes in bed. *Crunch, crunch, crunch,* all night—*crunch, crunch, crunch.*" I giggled, and the tall man looked over at us from where he was washing a pan in the stream. The last of the sunlight was on him, and those green eyes were bright as new leaves. One of them winked at me, and I *felt* it, the way you feel a tiny breeze on your skin when it's hot.

Then he went back to scrubbing the pan.

"Will it take us long to reach the king?" I asked her. "You said he didn't live too far, and I'm scared the griffin will eat somebody else while I'm gone. I need to be home."

Molly finished with my hair and gave it a gentle tug in back to bring my head up and make me look straight into her eyes. They were as gray as Schmendrick's were green, and I already knew that they turned darker or lighter gray depending on her mood. "What do you expect to happen when you meet King Lír, Sooz?" she asked me right back. "What did you have in mind when you set off to find him?"

I was surprised. "Well, I'm going to get him to come back to my village with me. All those knights he keeps sending aren't doing any good at all, so he'll just have to take care of that griffin himself. He's the king. It's his job."

"Yes," Molly said, but she said it so softly I could barely hear her. She patted my arm once, lightly, and then she got up and walked away to sit by herself near the fire. She made it look as though she was banking the fire, but she wasn't really.

We started out early the next morning. Molly had me in front of her on her horse for a time, but by and by Schmendrick took me up on his, to spare the other one's sore hoof. He was more comfortable to lean against than I'd expected—bony in some places, nice and springy in others. He didn't talk much, but he sang a lot as we went along, sometimes in languages I couldn't make out a word of, sometimes making up silly songs to make me laugh, like this one:

Soozli, Soozli, speaking loozli,
you disturb my oozli-goozli.
Soozli, Soozli,
would you choozli
to become my squoozli-squoozli?

He didn't do anything magic, except maybe once, when a crow kept diving at the horse—out of meanness; that's all, there wasn't a nest anywhere—making the poor thing dance and shy and skitter until I almost fell off. Schmendrick finally turned in the saddle and *looked* at it, and the next minute a hawk came swooping out of nowhere and chased that crow screaming into a thornbush where the hawk couldn't follow. I guess that was magic.

It was actually pretty country we were passing through, once we got onto the proper road. Trees, meadows, little soft valleys, hillsides covered with wildflowers I didn't know. You could see they got a lot more rain here than we do where I live. It's a good thing sheep don't need grazing, the way cows do. They'll go where the goats go, and goats will go anywhere. We're like that in my village, we have to be. But I liked this land better.

Schmendrick told me it hadn't always been like that. "Before Lír, this was all barren desert where nothing grew—*nothing*, Sooz. It was said that the country was under a curse, and in a way it was, but I'll tell you about that another time." People *always* say that when you're a child, and I hate it. "But Lír changed everything. The land was so glad to see him that it began blooming and blossoming the moment he became king, and it has done so ever since. Except poor Hagsgate, but that's another story, too." His voice got slower and deeper when he talked about Hagsgate, as though he weren't talking to me.

I twisted my neck around to look up at him. "Do you think King Lír will come back with me and kill that griffin? I think Molly thinks he won't, because he's so old." I hadn't known I was worried about that until I actually said it.

"Why, of course he will, girl." Schmendrick winked at me again. "He never could resist the plea of a maiden in distress, the more difficult and dangerous the deed, the better. If he did not spur to your village's aid himself at the first call, it was surely because he was engaged on some other heroic venture. I'm as certain as I can be that as soon as you make your request—remember to curtsy properly—he'll snatch up his great sword and spear, whisk you up to his saddlebow, and be off after your griffin with the road smoking behind him. Young or old, that's always been his way." He rumpled my hair in the back. "Molly overworries. That's *her* way. We are who we are."

"What's a curtsy?" I asked him. I know now, because Molly showed me, but I didn't then. He didn't laugh, except with his eyes, then gestured for me to face forward again as he went back to singing.

Soozli, Soozli, you amuse me,
right down to my solesli-shoesli.
Soozli, Soozli,
I bring newsli—
we could wed next stewsli-Tuesli.

I learned that the king had lived in a castle on a cliff by the sea when he was young, less than a day's journey from Hagsgate, but it fell down—Schmendrick wouldn't tell me how—so he built a new one somewhere else. I was sorry about that, because I've never seen the sea, and I've always wanted to, and I still haven't. But I'd never seen a castle, either, so there was that. I leaned back against his chest and fell asleep.

They'd been traveling slowly, taking time to let Molly's horse heal, but once its hoof was all right we galloped most of the rest of the way. Those horses of theirs didn't look magic or special, but they could run for hours without getting tired, and when I helped to rub them down and curry them, they were hardly sweating. They slept on their sides, like people, not standing up, the way our horses do.

Even so, it took us three full days to reach King Lír. Molly said he had bad memories of the castle that fell down, so that was why this one was as far from the sea as he could make it, and as different from the old one. It was on a hill, so the king could see anyone coming along the road, but there wasn't a moat, and there weren't any guards in armor, and there was only one banner on the walls. It was blue, with a picture of a white unicorn on it. Nothing else.

I was disappointed. I tried not to show it, but Molly saw. "You wanted a fortress," she said to me gently. "You were expecting dark stone towers, flags and cannons and knights, trumpeters blowing from the battlements. I'm sorry. It being your first castle, and all."

"No, it's a *pretty* castle," I said. And it *was* pretty, sitting peacefully on its hilltop in the sunlight, surrounded by all those wildflowers. There was a marketplace, I could see now, and there were huts like ours snugged up against the castle walls, so that the people could come inside for protection, if they needed to. I said, "Just looking at it, you can see that the king is a nice man."

Molly was looking at me with her head a little bit to one side. She said, "He is a hero, Sooz. Remember that, whatever else you see, whatever you think. Lír is a hero."

"Well, I know *that*," I said. "I'm sure he'll help me. I am."

But I wasn't. The moment I saw that nice, friendly castle, I wasn't a bit sure.

We didn't have any trouble getting in. The gate simply opened when Schmendrick knocked once, and he and Molly and I walked in through the market, where people were selling all kinds of fruits and vegetables, pots and pans and clothing and so on, the way they do in our village. They all called to us to come over to their barrows and buy things, but nobody tried to stop us going into the castle. There were two men at the two great doors, and they did ask us our names and why we wanted to see King Lír. The moment Schmendrick told them his name, they stepped back quickly and let us by, so I began to think that maybe he actually was a great magician, even if I never saw him do anything but little tricks and little songs. The men didn't offer to take him to the king, and he didn't ask.

Molly was right. I *was* expecting the castle to be all cold and shadowy, with queens looking sideways at us and big men clanking by in armor. But the halls we followed Schmendrick through were full of sunlight from long, high windows, and the people we saw mostly nodded and smiled at us. We passed a stone stair curling up out of sight, and I was sure that the king must live at the top, but Schmendrick never looked at it. He led us straight through the great hall—they had a fireplace big enough to roast three cows!—and on past the kitchens and the scullery and the laundry, to a room under another stair. *That* was dark. You wouldn't have found it unless you knew where to look. Schmendrick didn't knock at that door, and he didn't say anything magic to make it open. He just stood outside and waited, and by and by it rattled open, and we went in.

The king was in there. All by himself, the king was in there.

He was sitting on an ordinary wooden chair, not a throne. It was a really small room, the same size as my mother's weaving room, so maybe that's why he looked so big. He was as tall as Schmendrick, but he seemed so much *wider*. I was ready for him to have a long beard, spreading out all across his chest, but he only had a short one, like my father, except white. He wore a red and gold mantle, and there was a real golden crown on his white head, not much bigger than the wreaths we put on our champion rams at the end of the year. He had a kind face, with a big old nose, and big blue eyes, like a little boy. But his eyes were so tired and heavy, I didn't know how he kept them open. Sometimes he didn't. There was nobody else in the little room, and he peered at the three of us as though he knew he knew us, but not *why*. He tried to smile.

Schmendrick said very gently, "Majesty, it is Schmendrick and Molly, Molly Grue." The king blinked at him.

"Molly with the cat," Molly whispered. "You remember the cat, Lír."

"Yes," the king said. It seemed to take him forever to speak that one word. "The cat, yes, of course." But he didn't say anything after that, and we stood there and stood there, and the king kept smiling at something I couldn't see.

Schmendrick said to Molly, "*She* used to forget herself like that." His voice had changed, the same way it changed when he was talking about the way the land used to be. He said, "And then you would always remind her that she was a unicorn."

And the king changed, too, then. All at once his eyes were clear and shining with feeling, like Molly's eyes, and he *saw* us for the first time. He said softly, "Oh, my friends!" and he stood up and came to us and put his arms around Schmendrick and Molly. And I saw that he had been a hero, and that he was still a hero, and I began to think it might be all right, after all. Maybe it was really going to be all right.

"And who may this princess be?" he asked, looking straight at me. He had the proper voice for a king, deep and strong, but not frightening, not mean. I tried to tell him my name, but I couldn't make a sound, so he actually knelt on one knee in front of me, and he took my hand. He said, "I have often been of some use to princesses in distress. Command me."

"I'm not a princess, I'm Sooz," I said, "and I'm from a village you wouldn't even know, and there's a griffin eating the children." It all tumbled out like that, in one breath, but he didn't laugh or look at me any differently. What he did was ask me the name of my village, and I told him, and he said, "But indeed I know it, madam. I have been there. And now I will have the pleasure of returning."

Over his shoulder I saw Schmendrick and Molly staring at each other. Schmendrick was about to say something, but then they both turned toward the door, because a small dark woman, about my mother's age, only dressed in tunic, trews, and boots like Molly, had just come in. She said in a small, worried voice, "I am so truly sorry that I was not here to greet His Majesty's old companions. No need to tell me your illustrious names—my own is Lisene, and I am the king's royal secretary, translator, and protector." She took King Lír's arm, very politely and carefully, and began moving him back to his chair.

Schmendrick seemed to take a minute getting his own breath back. He said, "I have never known my old friend Lír to need any of those services. Especially a protector."

Lisene was busy with the king and didn't look at Schmendrick as she answered him. "How long has it been since you saw him last?" Schmendrick didn't answer. Lisene's voice was quiet still, but not so nervous. "Time sets its claw in us all, my lord, sooner or later. We are none of us that which we were." King Lír sat down obediently on his chair and closed his eyes.

I could tell that Schmendrick was angry, and growing angrier as he stood there, but he didn't show it. My father gets angry like that, which is how I knew. He said, "His Majesty has agreed to return to this young person's village with her, in order to rid her people of a marauding griffin. We will start out tomorrow."

Lisene swung around on us so fast that I was sure she was going to start shouting and giving everybody orders. But she didn't do anything like that. You could never have told that she was the least bit annoyed or alarmed. All she said was, "I am afraid that will not be possible, my lord. The king is in no fit condition for such a journey, nor certainly for such a deed."

"The king thinks rather differently." Schmendrick was talking through clenched teeth now.

"Does he, then?" Lisene pointed at King Lír, and I saw that he had fallen asleep in his chair. His head was drooping—I was afraid his crown was going to fall off—and his mouth hung open. Lisene said, "You came seeking the peerless warrior you remember, and you have found a spent, senile old man. Believe me, I understand your distress, but you must see—"

Schmendrick cut her off. I never understood what people meant when they talked about someone's eyes actually flashing, but at least green eyes can do it. He looked even taller than he was, and when he pointed a finger at Lisene I honestly expected the small woman to catch fire or maybe melt away. Schmendrick's voice was especially frightening because it was so quiet. He said, "Hear me now. I am Schmendrick the Magician, and I see my old friend Lír, as I have always seen him, wise and powerful and good, beloved of a unicorn."

And with that word, for a second time, the king woke up. He blinked once, then gripped the arms of the chair and pushed himself to his feet. He didn't look at us, but at Lisene, and he said, "I will go with them. It is my task and my gift. You will see to it that I am made ready."

Lisene said, "Majesty, no! Majesty, I beg you!"

King Lír reached out and took Lisene's head between his big hands, and I saw that there was love between them. He said, "It is what I am for. You know that as well as *he* does. See to it, Lisene, and keep all well for me while I am gone."

Lisene looked so sad, so *lost*, that I didn't know what to think, about her or King Lír or anything. I didn't realize that I had moved back against Molly Grue until I felt her hand in my hair. She didn't say anything, but it was nice smelling her there. Lisene said, very quietly, "I will see to it."

She turned around then and started for the door with her head lowered. I think she wanted to pass us by without looking at us at all, but she couldn't do it. Right at the door, her head came up and she stared at Schmendrick so hard that I pushed into Molly's skirt so I couldn't see her eyes. I heard her say, as though she could barely make the words come out, "His death be on your head, magician." I think she was crying, only not, the way grown people do.

And I heard Schmendrick's answer, and his voice was so cold I wouldn't have recognized it if I didn't know. "He has died before. Better that death—better this, better *any* death—than the one he was dying in that chair. If the griffin kills him, it will yet have saved his life." I heard the door close.

I asked Molly, speaking as low as I could, "What did he mean, about the king having died?" But she put me to one side, and she went to King Lír and knelt in front of him, reaching up to take one of his hands between hers. She said, "Lord . . . Majesty . . . friend . . . dear friend— remember. Oh, please, please *remember*."

The old man was swaying on his feet, but he put his other hand on Molly's head and he mumbled, "Child, Sooz—is that your pretty name, Sooz?—of course I will come to your village. The griffin was never hatched that dares harm King Lír's people." He sat down hard in the chair again, but he held on to her hand tightly. He looked at her, with his blue eyes wide and his mouth trembling a little. He said, "But you must remind me, little one. When I . . . when I lose myself—when I lose *her*—you must remind me that I am still searching, still waiting . . . that I have never forgotten her, never turned from all she taught me. I sit in this place . . . I *sit* . . . because a king has to sit, you see . . . but in my mind, in my poor mind, I am always away with *her*."

I didn't have any idea what he was talking about. I do now.

He fell asleep again then, holding Molly's hand. She sat with him for a long time, resting her head on his knee. Schmendrick went off to make sure Lisene was doing what she was supposed to do, getting everything ready for the king's departure. There was a lot of clattering and shouting already, enough so you'd have thought a war was starting, but nobody came in to see King Lír or speak to him, wish him luck or anything. It was almost as though he wasn't really there.

Me, I tried to write a letter home, with pictures of the king and the castle, but I fell asleep like him, and I slept the rest of that day and all night, too. I woke up in a bed I couldn't remember getting into, with Schmendrick looking down at me, saying, "Up, child, on your feet. You started all this uproar—it's time for you to see it through. The king is coming to slay your griffin."

I was out of bed before he'd finished speaking. I said, "Now? Are we going right now?"

Schmendrick shrugged his shoulders. "By noon, anyway, if I can finally get Lisene and the rest of them to understand that they are *not* coming. Lisene wants to bring fifty men-at-arms, a dozen wagonloads of supplies, a regiment of runners to send messages back and forth, and every wretched physician in the kingdom." He sighed and spread his hands. "I may have to turn the lot of them to stone if we are to be off today."

I thought he was probably joking, but I already knew that you couldn't be sure with Schmendrick. He said, "If Lír comes with a train of followers, there will be no Lír. Do you understand me, Sooz?" I shook my head. Schmendrick said, "It is my fault. If I had made sure to visit here more often, there were things I could have done to restore the Lír Molly and I once knew. My fault, my thoughtlessness."

I remembered Molly telling me, "Schmendrick has trouble with time." I still didn't know what she meant, nor this, either. I said, "It's just the way old people get. We have old men in our village who talk like him. One woman, too, Mam Jennet. She always cries when it rains."

Schmendrick clenched his fist and pounded it against his leg. "King Lír is *not* mad, girl, nor is he senile, as Lisene called him. He is *Lír*, Lír still, I promise you that. It is only here, in this castle, surrounded by good, loyal people who love him—who will love him to death, if they are allowed—that he sinks into . . . into the condition you have seen." He didn't say anything more for a moment; then he stooped a little to peer closely at me. "Did you notice the change in him when I spoke of unicorns?"

"Unicorn," I answered. "One unicorn who loved him. I noticed."

Schmendrick kept looking at me in a new way, as though we'd never met before. He said, "Your pardon, Sooz. I keep taking you for a child. Yes. One unicorn. He has not seen her since he became king, but he is what he is because of her. And when I speak that word, when Molly or I say her name—which I have not done yet— then he is recalled to himself." He paused for a moment, and then added, very softly, "As we had so often to do for her, so long ago."

"I didn't know unicorns had names," I said. "I didn't know they ever loved people."

"They don't. Only this one." He turned and walked away swiftly, saying over his shoulder, "Her name was Amalthea. Go find Molly, she'll see you fed."

The room I'd slept in wasn't big, not for something in a castle. Catania, the headwoman of our village, has a bedroom nearly as large, which I know because I play with her daughter Sophia. But the sheets I'd been under were embroidered with a crown, and engraved on the headboard was a picture of the blue banner with the white unicorn. I had slept the night in King Lír's own bed while he dozed in an old wooden chair.

I didn't wait to have breakfast with Molly, but ran straight to the little room where I had last seen the king.

He was there, but so changed that I froze in the doorway, trying to get my breath. Three men were bustling around him like tailors, dressing him in his armor: all the padding underneath, first, and then the different pieces for the arms and legs and shoulders. I don't know any of the names. The men hadn't put his helmet on him, so his head stuck out at the top, white-haired and big-nosed and blue-eyed, but he didn't look silly like that. He looked like a giant.

When he saw me, he smiled, and it was a warm, happy smile, but it was a little frightening, too, almost a little terrible, like the time I saw the griffin burning in the black sky. It was a hero's smile. I'd never seen one before. He called to me, "Little one, come and buckle on my sword, if you would. It would be an honor for me."

The men had to show me how you do it. The sword belt, all by itself, was so heavy it kept slipping through my fingers, and I did need help with the buckle. But I put the sword into its sheath alone, although I needed both hands to lift it. When it slid home it made a sound like a great door slamming shut. King Lír touched my face with one of his cold iron gloves and said, "Thank you, little one. The next time that blade is drawn, it will be to free your village. You have my word."

Schmendrick came in then, took one look, and just shook his head. He said, "This is the most ridiculous. . . . It is four days' ride—perhaps five—with the weather turning hot enough to broil a lobster on an iceberg. There's no need for armor until he faces the griffin." You could see how stupid he felt they all were, but King Lír smiled at him the same way he'd smiled at me, and Schmendrick stopped talking.

King Lír said, "Old friend, I go forth as I mean to return. It is my way."

Schmendrick looked like a little boy himself for a moment. All he could say was, "Your business. Don't blame me, that's all. At *least* leave the helmet off."

He was about to turn away and stalk out of the room, but Molly came up behind him and said, "Oh, Majesty— Lír—how grand! How beautiful you are!" She sounded the way my aunt Zerelda sounds when she's carrying on about my brother, Wilfrid. He could mess his pants and jump in a hog pen, and Aunt Zerelda would still think he was the best, smartest boy in the whole world. But Molly was different. She brushed those tailors, or whatever they were, straight aside, and she stood on tiptoe to smooth King Lír's white hair, and I heard her whisper, "I wish *she* could see you."

King Lír looked at her for a long time without saying anything. Schmendrick stood there, off to the side, and he didn't say anything, either, but they were together, the three of them. I wish that Felicitas and I could have been together like that when we got old. Could have had time.

Then King Lír looked at *me*, and he said, "The child is

waiting." And that's how we set off for home. The king, Schmendrick, Molly, and me.

To the last minute, poor old Lisene kept trying to get King Lír to take some knights or soldiers with him. She actually followed us on foot when we left, calling, "Highness—Majesty—if you will have none else, take me! Take me!" At that the king stopped and turned and went back to her. He got down off his horse and embraced Lisene, and I don't know what they said to each other, but Lisene didn't follow anymore after that.

I rode with the king most of the time, sitting up in front of him on his skittery black mare. I wasn't sure I could trust her not to bite me or to kick me when I wasn't looking, but King Lír told me, "It is only peaceful times that make her nervous, be assured of that. When dragons charge her, belching death—for the fumes are more dangerous than the flames, little one—when your griffin swoops down at her, you will see her at her best." I still didn't like her much, but I did like the king. He didn't sing to me, the way Schmendrick had, but he told me stories, and they weren't fables or fairy tales. These were real, true stories, and he knew they were true because they had all happened to him! I never heard stories like those, and I never will again. I know that for certain.

He told me more things to keep in mind if you have to fight a dragon, and he told me how he learned that ogres aren't always as stupid as they look, and why you should

never swim in a mountain pool when the snows are melting, and how you can *sometimes* make friends with a troll.
He talked about his father's castle, where he grew up, and
about how he met Schmendrick and Molly there, and
even about Molly's cat, which he said was a little thing
with a funny crooked ear. But when I asked him why the
castle fell down, he wouldn't exactly say, no more than
Schmendrick would. His voice became very quiet and faraway. "I forget things, you know, little one," he said. "I try
to hold on, but I do forget."

Well, I knew *that*. He kept calling Molly Sooz, and he
never called me anything but *little one*, and Schmendrick
kept having to remind him where we were bound and
why. That was always at night, though. He was usually
fine during the daytime. And when he did turn confused
again, and wander off (not just in his mind, either—I
found him in the woods one night, talking to a tree as
though it was his father), all you had to do was mention a
white unicorn named Amalthea, and he'd come to himself almost right away. Generally it was Schmendrick who
did that, but I brought him back that time, holding my
hand and telling me how you can recognize a pooka, and
why you need to. But I could never get him to say a word
about the unicorn.

Autumn comes early where I live. The days were still
hot, and the king never would take his armor off, except
to sleep, not even his helmet with the big blue plume on

top, but at night I burrowed in between Molly and Schmendrick for warmth, and you could hear the stags belling everywhere all the time, crazy with the season. One of them actually charged King Lír's horse while I was riding with him, and Schmendrick was about to do something magic to the stag, the same way he'd done with the crow. But the king laughed and rode straight at him, right *into* those horns. I screamed, but the black mare never hesitated, and the stag turned at the last moment and ambled out of sight in the brush. He was wagging his tail in circles, the way goats do, and looking as puzzled and dreamy as King Lír himself.

I was proud, once I got over being frightened. But both Schmendrick and Molly scolded him, and he kept apologizing to me for the rest of the day for having put me in danger, as Molly had once said he would. "I forgot you were with me, little one, and for that I will always ask your pardon." Then he smiled at me with that beautiful, terrible hero's smile I'd seen before, and he said, "But oh, little one, the remembering!" And that night he didn't wander away and get himself lost. Instead he sat happily by the fire with us and sang a whole long song about the adventures of an outlaw called Captain Cully. I'd never heard of him, but it's a really good song.

We reached my village late on the afternoon of the fourth day, and Schmendrick made us stop together before we rode in. He said, directly to me, "Sooz, if you tell them that this is the king himself, there will be nothing but noise and joy and celebration, and nobody will get any rest with all that carrying-on. It would be best for you to tell them that we have brought King Lír's greatest knight with us, and that he needs a night to purify himself in prayer and meditation before he deals with your griffin." He took hold of my chin and made me look into his green, green eyes, and he said, "Girl, you have to trust me. I always know what I'm doing—that's my trouble. Tell your people what I've said." And Molly touched me and looked at me without saying anything, so I knew it was all right.

I left them camped on the outskirts of the village, and walked home by myself. Malka met me first. She smelled me before I even reached Simon and Elsie's tavern, and she came running and crashed into my legs and knocked me over, and then pinned me down with her paws on my shoulders, and kept licking my face until I had to nip her nose to make her let me up and run to the house with me. My father was out with the flock, but my mother and Wilfrid were there, and they grabbed me and nearly strangled me, and they cried over me—rotten, stupid Wilfrid, too!—because everyone had been so certain that I'd been taken and eaten by the griffin. After that, once she got done crying, my mother spanked me for running off in Uncle Ambrose's cart without telling anyone, and when my father came in, he spanked me all over again. But I didn't mind.

I told them I'd seen King Lír in person, and been in his castle, and I said what Schmendrick had told me to say, but nobody was much cheered by it. My father just sat down and grunted, "Oh, aye—another great warrior for our comfort and the griffin's dessert. Your bloody king won't ever come here his bloody self, you can be sure of that." My mother reproached him for talking like that in front of Wilfrid and me, but he went on. "Maybe he cared about places like this, people like us once, but he's old now, and old kings only care who's going to be king after them. You can't tell me anything different."

I wanted more than anything to tell him that King Lír *was* here, less than half a mile from our doorstep, but I didn't, and not only because Schmendrick had told me not to. I wasn't sure what the king might look like, white-haired and shaky and not here all the time, to people like my father. I wasn't sure what he looked like to me, for that matter. He was a lovely, dignified old man who told wonderful stories, but when I tried to imagine him riding alone into the Midwood to do battle with a griffin, a griffin that had already eaten his best knights . . . to be honest, I couldn't do it. Now that I'd actually brought him all the way home with me, as I'd set out to do, I was suddenly afraid that I'd drawn him to his death. And I knew I wouldn't ever forgive myself if that happened.

I wanted so much to see them that night, Schmendrick and Molly and the king. I wanted to sleep out there on the ground with them, and listen to their talk, and then maybe I'd not worry so much about the morning. But of course there wasn't a chance of that. My family would hardly let me out of their sight to wash my face. Wilfrid kept following me around, asking endless questions about the castle, and my father took me to Catania, who had me tell the whole story over again, and agreed with him that whomever the king had sent this time wasn't likely to be any more use than the others had been. And my mother kept feeding me and scolding me and hugging me, all more or less at the same time. And then, in the night, we heard the griffin, making that soft, lonely, horrible sound it makes when it's hunting. So I didn't get very much sleep, between one thing and another.

But at sunrise, after I'd helped Wilfrid milk the goats, they let me run out to the camp, as long as Malka came with me, which was practically like having my mother along. Molly was already helping King Lír into his armor, and Schmendrick was burying the remains of last night's dinner, as though they were starting one more ordinary day on their journey to somewhere. They greeted me, and Schmendrick thanked me for doing as he'd asked, so that the king could have a restful night before he—

I didn't let him finish. I didn't know I was going to do it, I swear, but I ran up to King Lír, and I threw my arms around him, and I said, "Don't go! I changed my mind, don't go!" Just like Lisene.

King Lír looked down at me. He seemed as tall as a tree right then, and he patted my head very gently with his iron glove. He said, "Little one, I have a griffin to slay. It is my job."

Which was what I'd said myself, though it seemed like years ago, and that made it so much worse. I said a second time, "I changed my mind! Somebody else can fight the griffin, you don't have to! You go home! You go home *now* and live your life, and be the king, and everything. . . ." I was babbling and sniffling, and generally being a baby, I know that. I'm glad Wilfrid didn't see me.

King Lír kept petting me with one hand and trying to put me aside with the other, but I wouldn't let go. I think I was actually trying to pull his sword out of its sheath, to take it away from him. He said, "No, no, little one, you don't understand. There are some monsters that only a king can kill. I have always known that—I should never, never have sent those poor men to die in my place. No one else in all the land can do this for you and your village. Most truly now, it is my job." And he kissed my hand, the way he must have kissed the hands of so many queens. He kissed my hand, too, just like theirs.

Molly came up then and took me away from him. She held me close, and she stroked my hair, and she told me, "Child, Sooz, there's no turning back for him now, or for you, either. It was your fate to bring this last cause to him, and his fate to take it up, and neither of you could have done differently, being who you are. And now you must be as brave as he is, and see it all play out." She caught herself there, and changed it. "Rather, you must wait to learn how it has played out, because you are certainly not coming into that forest with us."

"I'm coming," I said. "You can't stop me. Nobody can." I wasn't sniffling or anything anymore. I said it like that, that's all.

Molly held me at arm's length, and she shook me a little bit. She said, "Sooz, if you can tell me that your parents have given their permission, then you may come. Have they done so?"

I didn't answer her. She shook me again, gentler this time, saying, "Oh, that was wicked of me, forgive me, my dear friend. I knew the day we met that you could never learn to lie." Then she took both of my hands between hers, and she said, "Lead us to the Midwood, if you will, Sooz, and we will say our farewells there. Will you do that for us? For me?"

I nodded, but I still didn't speak. I couldn't, my throat was hurting so much. Molly squeezed my hands and said, "Thank you." Schmendrick came up and made some kind of sign to her with his eyes, or his eyebrows, because she said, "Yes, I know," although he hadn't said a thing. So she went to King Lír with him, and I was alone, trying to stop shaking. I managed it, after a while.

The Midwood isn't far. They wouldn't really have

needed my help to find it. You can see the beginning of it from the roof of Ellis the baker's house, which is the tallest one on that side of the village. It's always dark, even from a distance, even if you're not actually in it. I don't know if that's because they're oak trees (we have all sorts of tales and sayings about oaken woods, and the creatures that live there) or maybe because of some enchantment, or because of the griffin.

Maybe it was different before the griffin came. Uncle Ambrose says it's been a bad place all his life; but my father says no, he and his friends used to hunt there, and he actually picnicked there once or twice with my mother, when they were young.

King Lír rode in front, looking grand and almost young, with his head up and the blue plume on his helmet floating above him, more like a banner than a feather. I was going to ride with Molly, but the king leaned from his saddle as I started past, and swooped me up before him, saying, "You shall guide and company me, little one, until we reach the forest." I was proud of that, but I was frightened, too, because he was so happy, and I knew he was going to his death, trying to make up for all those knights he'd sent to fight the griffin. I didn't try to warn him. He wouldn't have heard me, and I knew that, too. Me and poor old Lisene.

He told me all about griffins as we rode. He said, "If you should ever have dealings with a griffin, little one, you must remember that they are not like dragons. A dragon is simply a dragon—make yourself small when it dives down at you, but hold your ground and strike at the underbelly, and you've won the day. But a griffin, now . . . a griffin is two highly dissimilar creatures, eagle and lion, fused together by some god with a god's sense of humor. And so there is an eagle's heart beating in the beast, and a lion's heart as well, and you must pierce them both to have any hope of surviving the battle." He was as cheerful as he could be about it all, holding me safe on the saddle, and saying over and over, the way old people do, "Two hearts, never forget that—many people do. Eagle heart, lion heart—eagle heart, lion heart. *Never* forget, little one."

We passed a lot of people I knew, out with their sheep and goats, and they all waved to me, and called, and made jokes, and so on. They cheered for King Lír, but they didn't bow to him, or take off their caps, because nobody recognized him, nobody knew. He seemed delighted about that, which most kings probably wouldn't be. But he's the only king I've met, so I can't say.

The Midwood seemed to be reaching out for us before we were anywhere near it, long fingery shadows stretching across the empty fields, and the leaves flickering and blinking, though there wasn't any wind. A forest is usually really noisy, day and night, if you stand still and listen to the birds and the insects and the streams and such, but the Midwood is always silent, silent. That reaches out, too, the silence.

We halted a stone's throw from the forest, and King Lír said to me, "We part here, little one," and set me down on the ground as carefully as though he was putting a bird back in its nest. He said to Schmendrick, "I know better than to try to keep you and Sooz from following"—he kept on calling Molly by my name, every time, I don't know why—"but I enjoin you, in the name of great Nikos himself, and in the name of our long and precious friendship."

He stopped there, and he didn't say anything more for such a while that I was afraid he was back to forgetting who he was and why he was there, the way he had been. But then he went on, clear and ringing as one of those mad stags, "I charge you in *her* name, in the name of the Lady Amalthea, not to assist me in any way from the moment we pass the very first tree, but to leave me altogether to what is mine to do. Is that understood between us, dear ones of my heart?"

Schmendrick hated it. You didn't have to be magic to see that. It was so plain, even to me, that he had been planning to take over the battle as soon as they were actually facing the griffin. But King Lír was looking right at him with those young blue eyes, and with a little bit of a smile on his face, and Schmendrick simply didn't know what to do. There wasn't anything he *could* do, so he finally nodded and mumbled, "If that is Your Majesty's wish." The king couldn't hear him at all the first time, so he made him say it again.

And then, of course, everybody had to say goodbye to me, since I wasn't allowed to go any farther with them. Molly said she knew we'd see each other again, and Schmendrick told me that I had the makings of a real warrior queen, only he was certain I was too smart to be one. And King Lír . . . King Lír said to me, very quietly, so nobody else could hear, "Little one, if I had married and had a daughter, I would have asked no more than that she should be as brave and kind and loyal as you. Remember that, as I will remember you to my last day."

Which was all nice, and I wished my mother and father could have heard what all these grown people were saying about me. But then they turned and rode on into the Mid- wood, the three of them, and only Molly looked back at me. And I think *that* was to make sure I wasn't following, because I was supposed just to go home and wait to find out if my friends were alive or dead, and if the griffin was going to be eating any more children. It was all over.

And maybe I would have gone home and let it be all over, if it hadn't been for Malka.

She should have been with the sheep and not with me, of course—that's her job, the same way King Lír was doing his job, going to meet the griffin. But Malka thinks I'm a sheep, too, the most stupid, aggravating sheep she

49

ever had to guard, forever wandering away into some kind of danger. All the way to the Midwood she had trotted quietly alongside the king's horse, but now that we were alone again she came rushing up and bounced all over me, barking like thunder and knocking me down, hard, the way she does whenever I'm not where she wants me to be. I always brace myself when I see her coming, but it never helps.

What she does then, before I'm on my feet, is take the hem of my smock in her jaws and start tugging me in the direction she thinks I should go. But this time . . . this time she suddenly got up, as though she'd forgotten all about me, and she stared past me at the Midwood with all the white showing in her eyes and a low sound coming out of her that I don't think she knew she could make. The next moment, she was gone, racing into the forest with foam flying from her mouth and her big ragged ears flat back. I called, but she couldn't have heard me, baying and barking the way she was.

Well, I didn't have any choice. King Lír and Schmendrick and Molly all had a choice, going after the Midwood griffin, but Malka was my dog, and she didn't know what she was facing, and I *couldn't* let her face it by herself. So there wasn't anything else for me to do. I took an enormous long breath and looked around me, and then I walked into the forest after her.

Actually, I ran, as long as I could, and then I walked

until I could run again, and then I ran some more. There aren't any paths into the Midwood, because nobody goes there, so it wasn't hard to see where three horses had pushed through the undergrowth, and then a dog's tracks on top of the hoofprints. It was very quiet with no wind, not one bird calling, no sound but my own panting. I couldn't even hear Malka anymore. I was hoping that maybe they'd come on the griffin while it was asleep, and King Lír had already killed it in its nest. I didn't think so, though. He'd probably have decided it wasn't honorable to attack a sleeping griffin, and wakened it up for a fair fight. I hadn't known him very long, but I knew what he'd do.

Then, a little way ahead of me, the whole forest exploded.

It was too much noise for me to sort it out in my head. There was Malka absolutely *howling*, and birds bursting up everywhere out of the brush, and Schmendrick or the king or someone was shouting, only I couldn't make out any of the words. And underneath it all was something that wasn't loud at all, a sound somewhere between a growl and that terrible soft call, like a frightened child. Then—just as I broke into the clearing—the rattle and scrape of knives, only much louder this time, as the griffin shot straight up with the sun on its wings. Its cold golden eyes *bit* into mine, and its beak was open so wide you could see down and down the blazing red gullet. It filled the sky.

And King Lír, astride his black mare, filled the clearing. He was as huge as the griffin, and his sword was the size of a boar spear, and he shook it at the griffin, daring it to light down and fight him on the ground. But the griffin was staying out of range, circling overhead to get a good look at these strange new people. Malka was utterly off her head, screaming and hurling herself into the air again and again, snapping at the griffin's lion feet and eagle claws, but coming down each time without so much as an iron feather between her teeth. I lunged and caught her in the air, trying to drag her away before the griffin turned on her, but she fought me, scratching my face with her own dull dog claws, until I had to let her go. The last time she leaped, the griffin suddenly stooped and caught her full on her side with one huge wing, so hard that she couldn't get a sound out, no more than I could. She flew all the way across the clearing, slammed into a tree, fell to the ground, and after that she didn't move.

Molly told me later that that was when King Lír struck for the griffin's lion heart. I didn't see it. I was flying across the clearing myself, throwing myself over Malka, in case the griffin came after her again, and I didn't see anything except her staring eyes and the blood on her side. But I did hear the griffin's roar when it happened, and when I could turn my head, I saw the blood splashing along *its* side, and the back legs squinching up against its belly, the way you do when you're really hurting. King Lír shouted like a boy. He threw that great sword as high as the griffin, and snatched it back again, and then he charged toward the griffin as it wobbled lower and lower, with its crippled lion half dragging it out of the air. It landed with a saggy thump, just like Malka, and there was a moment when I was absolutely sure it was dead. I remember I was thinking, very far away, *This is good*, *I'm glad*, *I'm sure I'm glad*.

But Schmendrick was screaming at the king, "Two hearts! *Two hearts!*" until his voice split with it, and Molly was on me, trying to drag me away from the griffin, and *I* was hanging on to Malka—she'd gotten so *heavy*—and I don't know what else was happening right then, because all I was seeing and thinking about was Malka. And all I was feeling was her heart not beating under mine.

She guarded my cradle when I was born. I cut my teeth on her poor ears, and she never made one sound. My mother says so.

King Lír wasn't seeing or hearing any of us. There was nothing in the world for him but the griffin, which was flopping and struggling lopsidedly in the middle of the clearing. I couldn't help feeling sorry for it, even then, even after it had killed Malka and my friends, and all the sheep and goats, too, and I don't know how many else. And King Lír must have felt the same way, because he got down from his black mare and went straight up to the griffin, and he spoke to it, lowering his sword until the tip was on the ground. He said, "You were a noble and terrible adversary—surely the last such I will ever confront. We have accomplished what we were born to do, the two of us. I thank you for your death."

And on that last word, the griffin had him.

It was the eagle, lunging up at him, dragging the lion half along, the way I'd been dragging Malka's dead weight. King Lír stepped back, swinging the sword fast enough to take off the griffin's head, but it was faster than he was. That dreadful beak caught him at the waist, shearing through his armor the way an ax would smash through piecrust, and he doubled over without a sound that I heard, looking like wet wash on the line. There was blood, and worse, and I couldn't have said if he was dead or alive. I thought the griffin was going to bite him in two.

I shook loose from Molly. She was calling to Schmendrick to *do* something, but of course he couldn't, and she knew it, because he'd promised King Lír that he wouldn't interfere by magic, whatever happened. But I wasn't a magician, and I hadn't promised anything to anybody. I told Malka I'd be right back.

The griffin didn't see me coming. It was bending its head down over King Lír, hiding him with its wings. The lion part trailing along so limply in the dust made it more fearful to see, though I can't say why, and it was making a sort of cooing, purring sound all the time. I had a big rock in my left hand, and a dead branch in my right, and I was bawling something, but I don't remember what. You can scare wolves away from the flock sometimes if you run at them like that, determined.

I can throw things hard with either hand—Wilfrid found *that* out when I was still small—and the griffin looked up fast when the rock hit it on the side of its neck. It didn't like that, but it was too busy with King Lír to bother with me. I didn't think for a minute that my branch was going to be any use on even a half-dead griffin, but I threw it as far as I could, so that the griffin would look away for a moment, and as soon as it did I made a little run and a big sprawling dive for the hilt of the king's sword, which was sticking out under him where he'd fallen. I knew I could lift it because of having buckled it on him when we set out together.

But I couldn't get it free. He was too heavy, like Malka. But I wouldn't give up or let go. I kept pulling and pulling on that sword, and I didn't feel Molly pulling at *me* again, and I didn't notice the griffin starting to scrabble toward me over King Lír's body. I did hear Schmendrick, sounding a long way off, and I thought he was singing one of the nonsense songs he'd made up for me, only why would he be doing something like that just now? Then I did finally look up, to push my sweaty hair off my face, just before the griffin grabbed me up in one of its claws, yanking me

55

away from Molly to throw me down on top of King Lír. His armor was so cold against my cheek, it was as though the armor had died with him.

The griffin looked into my eyes. That was the worst of all, worse than the pain where the claw had me, worse than not seeing my parents and stupid Wilfrid anymore, worse than knowing that I hadn't been able to save either the king or Malka. Griffins can't talk (dragons do, but only to heroes, King Lír told me), but those golden eyes were saying into my eyes, "Yes, I will die soon, but you are all dead now, all of you, and I will pick your bones before the ravens have mine. And your folk will remember what I was, and what I did to them, when there is no one left in your vile, pitiful anthill who remembers your name. So I have won." And I knew it was true.

Then there wasn't anything but that beak and that burning gullet opening over me. Then there was.

I thought it was a cloud. I was so dazed and terrified that I really thought it was a white cloud, only traveling so low and so fast that it smashed the griffin off King Lír and away from me, and sent me tumbling into Molly's arms at the same time. She held me tightly, practically smothering me, and it wasn't until I wriggled my head free that I saw what had come to us. I can see it still, in my mind. I see it right now.

They don't look *anything* like horses. I don't know where people got that notion. Four legs and a tail, yes, but the hoofs are split, like a deer's hoofs, or a goat's, and the head is smaller and more—*pointy*—than a horse's head. And the whole body is different from a horse; it's like saying a snowflake looks like a cow. The horn looks too long and heavy for the body, you can't imagine how a neck that delicate can hold up a horn that size. But it can.

Schmendrick was on his knees, with his eyes closed and his lips moving, as though he was still singing. Molly kept whispering, "Amalthea . . . Amalthea . . ." not to me, not to anybody. The unicorn was facing the griffin across the king's body. Her front feet were skittering and dancing a little, but her back legs were setting themselves to charge, the way rams do. Only rams put their heads down, while the unicorn held her head high, so that the horn caught the sunlight and glowed like a seashell. She gave a cry that made me want to dive back into Molly's skirt and cover my ears, it was so raw and so . . . *hurt*. Then her head did go down.

Dying or not, the griffin put up a furious fight. It came hopping to meet the unicorn, but then it was out of the way at the last minute, with its bloody beak snapping at the unicorn's legs as it flashed by. But each time that happened, the unicorn would turn instantly, much quicker than a horse could have turned, and come charging back before the griffin could get itself braced again. It wasn't a bit fair, but I didn't feel sorry for the griffin anymore.

The last time, the unicorn slashed sideways with her

horn, using it like a club, and knocked the griffin clean off its feet. But it was up before the unicorn could turn, and it actually leaped into the air, dead lion half and all, just high enough to come down on the unicorn's back, raking with its eagle claws and trying to bite through the unicorn's neck, the way it did with King Lír. I screamed then, I couldn't help it, but the unicorn reared up until I thought it was going to go over backward, and she flung the griffin to the ground, whirled, and drove her horn straight through the iron feathers to the eagle heart. She trampled the body for a good while after, but she didn't need to.

Schmendrick and Molly ran to King Lír. They didn't look at the griffin, or even pay very much attention to the unicorn. I wanted to go to Malka, but I followed them to where he lay. I'd seen what the griffin had done to him, closer than they had, and I didn't see how he could still be alive. But he was, just barely. He opened his eyes when we knelt beside him, and he smiled so sweetly at us all, and he said, "Lisene? Lisene, I should have a bath, shouldn't I?"

I didn't cry. Molly didn't cry. Schmendrick did. He said, "No, Majesty. No, you do not need bathing, truly."

King Lír looked puzzled. "But I smell bad, Lisene. I think I must have wet myself." He reached for my hand and held it so hard. "Little one," he said. "Little one, I know you. Do not be ashamed of me because I am old."

I squeezed his hand back, as hard as I could. "Hello,

Your Majesty," I said. "Hello." I didn't know what else to say.

Then his face was suddenly young and happy and wonderful, and he was gazing far past me, reaching toward something with his eyes. I felt a breath on my shoulder, and I turned my head and saw the unicorn. She was bleeding from a lot of deep scratches and bites, especially around her neck, but all you could see in her dark eyes was King Lír. I moved aside so she could get to him, but when I turned back, the king was gone. I'm nine, almost ten. I know when people are gone.

The unicorn stood over King Lír's body for a long time. I went off after a while to sit beside Malka, and Molly came and sat with me. But Schmendrick stayed kneeling by King Lír, and he was talking to the unicorn. I couldn't hear what he was saying, but I could tell from his face that he was asking for something, a favor. My mother says she can always tell before I open my mouth. The unicorn wasn't answering, of course—they can't talk, either, I'm almost sure—but Schmendrick kept at it until the unicorn turned its head and looked at him. Then he stopped, and he stood up and walked away by himself. The unicorn stayed where she was.

Molly was saying how brave Malka had been, and telling me that she'd never known another dog who attacked a griffin. She asked if Malka had ever had pups, and I said, yes, but none of them was Malka. It was very strange. She was trying hard to make me feel better, and I was trying to comfort her because she couldn't. But all the while I felt so cold, almost as far away from everything as Malka had gone. I closed her eyes, the way you do with people, and I sat there and I stroked her side, over and over.

I didn't notice the unicorn. Molly must have, but she didn't say anything. I went on petting Malka, and I didn't look up until the horn came slanting over my shoulder. Close to, you could see blood drying in the shining spirals, but I wasn't afraid. I wasn't anything. Then the horn touched Malka, very lightly, right where I was stroking her, and Malka opened her eyes.

It took her a while to understand that she was alive. It took me longer. She ran her tongue out first, panting and panting, looking so *thirsty*. We could hear a stream trickling somewhere close, and Molly went and found it, and brought water back in her cupped hands. Malka lapped it all up, and then she tried to stand and fell down, like a puppy. But she kept trying, and at last she was properly on her feet, and she tried to lick my face, but she missed it the first few times. I only started crying when she finally managed it.

When she saw the unicorn, she did a funny thing. She stared at her for a moment, and then Malka bowed or curtseyed, in a dog way, stretching out her front legs and putting her head down on the ground between them. The unicorn nosed at her, very gently, so as not to knock her over again. The unicorn looked at me for the first time . . . or maybe I really looked at *her* for the first time, past the horn and the hoofs and the magical whiteness, all the way into those endless eyes. And what they did, somehow, the unicorn's eyes, was to free me from the griffin's eyes. Because the awfulness of what I'd seen there didn't go away when the griffin died, not even when Malka came alive again. But the unicorn had all the world in her eyes, all the world I'm never going to see, but it doesn't matter, because now I *have* seen it, and it's beautiful, and I was in there, too.

And when I think of Jehane, and Louli, and my Felicitas who could only talk with her eyes, just like the unicorn, I'll think of them, and not the griffin. That's how it was when the unicorn and I looked at each other.

I didn't see if the unicorn said goodbye to Molly and Schmendrick, and I didn't see when it went away. I didn't want to. I did hear Schmendrick saying, "A dog. I nearly kill myself singing her to Lír, calling her as no other has *ever* called a unicorn—and she brings back, not him, but the dog. And here I'd always thought she had no sense of humor."

But Molly said, "She loved him, too. That's why she let him go. Keep your voice down." I was going to tell her it didn't matter, that I knew Schmendrick was saying that because he was so sad, but she came over and petted Malka with me, and I didn't have to. She said, "We will escort you and Malka home now, as befits two great ladies. Then we will take the king home, too."

"And I'll never see you again," I said. "No more than I'll see him."

Molly asked me, "How old are you, Sooz?"

"Nine," I said. "Almost ten. You know that."

"You can whistle?" I nodded. Molly looked around quickly, as though she were going to steal something. She bent close to me, and she whispered, "I will give you a present, Sooz, but you are not to open it until the day when you turn seventeen. On that day you must walk out away from your village, walk out all alone into some quiet place that is special to you, and you must whistle like this." And she whistled a little ripple of music for me to whistle back to her, repeating and repeating it until she was satisfied that I had it exactly. "Don't whistle it anymore," she told me. "Don't whistle it aloud again, not once, until your seventeenth birthday, but keep whistling it inside you. Do you understand the difference, Sooz?"

"I'm not a baby," I said. "I understand. What will happen when I do whistle it?"

Molly smiled at me. She said, "Someone will come to you. Maybe the greatest magician in the world, maybe only an old lady with a soft spot for valiant, impudent children." She cupped my cheek in her hand. "And just maybe even a unicorn. Because beautiful things will always want to see you again, Sooz, and be listening for you. Take an old lady's word for it. Someone will come."

They put King Lír on his own horse, and I rode with Schmendrick, and they came all the way home with me, right to the door, to tell my mother and father that the griffin was dead, and that I had helped, and you should have seen Wilfrid's face when they said *that*! Then they both hugged me, and Molly said in my ear, "Remember— not till you're seventeen!" and they rode away, taking the king back to his castle to be buried among his own folk. And I had a cup of cold milk and went out with Malka and my father to pen the flock for the night.

So that's what happened to me. I practice the music Molly taught me in my head, all the time, I even dream it some nights, but I don't ever whistle it aloud. I talk to Malka about our adventure, because I have to talk to *someone*. And I promise her that when the time comes she'll be there with me, in the special place I've already picked out. She'll be an old dog lady then, of course, but it doesn't matter. Someone will come to us both.

I hope it's them, those two. A unicorn is very nice, but they're my friends. I want to feel Molly holding me again, and hear the stories she didn't have time to tell me, and I want to hear Schmendrick singing that silly song:

Soozli, Soozli, speaking loozli,
you disturb my oozli-goozli.
Soozli, Soozli,
would you choozli
to become my squoozli-squoozli . . . ?

I can wait.

SOOZ

For my Nell

"with the love
that knows but cannot understand . . ."

I

MALKA WOKE ME ON THE MORNING OF MY seventeenth birthday, climbing into my bed and licking my face.

It was hard for her, because she was a very old dog now, and her back legs didn't really work anymore. My brother, Wilfrid, got married last Thieves' Day and moved to Gamladry, to be near his wife's family, and I'd been sleeping downstairs ever since. My mother wanted Malka to sleep in the kitchen, because of the way she was coming to smell, but I wouldn't have it. Malka was as beautiful as a unicorn to me. And I've seen a unicorn.

So has Malka. It was a unicorn that brought her back to life when she'd been killed by a griffin, defending me. To be honest, it was the magician who called the unicorn, and she came, and she trampled that griffin to a mash of rags and dust and iron feathers . . . and then she touched Malka with her horn, and she went away. And I'll have forgotten how magnificent she was—and how terrifying, so much more than the griffin—before I ever forget the wonder of Malka staggering to her feet, and falling down, and getting up, and by and by lapping water from Molly Grue's cupped hands. *Molly Grue* . . .

But what Malka came for just then was to remind me that today, my birthday, was the day when I was supposed to go off by myself and whistle. Molly told me so.

Molly's not a magician—that's Schmendrick—and she's not magically glorious, like a unicorn. She's just Molly, and her toes hurt whenever there's a storm coming, and I love her. Even though I haven't seen her since we all fought the griffin, and she hugged me goodbye and taught me a song. Not a song, really—just a silly bit of music that she made me whistle over and over and *over*, until it was as much part of me as my own name. And she told me that when I whistled that music, *someone* would come to me.

I hoped it would be her, or Schmendrick, but she said she didn't have any idea. Only that I had to be alone—without Malka, even—and that I mustn't be afraid. "Not that you would be," she added, with that small chuckle in her eyes that I've never seen since in any other eyes. "A girl who throws rocks at a griffin? Not likely, is it?" And she kissed me and rode away with Schmendrick, and Malka and I watched them all the way out of sight.

So first, after breakfast, with my mother gone to market, my father and I went out to pasture, to find out if any kids had been born during the night. Sheep have a season for birthing, and you can rely on it within a matter of days—as we would be doing very shortly—but goats are goats, and they drop their babies when they like. And *where*. They're like chickens that way—you have to track them and chase them through all manner of bushes and scrub and underbrush, where you can't believe any animal would ever think to hide a birth. I like goats better than sheep, but they're a trial.

We found three new kids, all healthy and nursing from mothers ready to take care of raising their children themselves, thank you very much. I held and stroked each of the kids for a while, so they'd know me again, while my father marked them with his own special crayon so that *he'd* know *them*. We have done this all my life, as long as I can remember.

I didn't like leaving Malka when I went off to meet whomever I was supposed to. I was afraid that she'd whine and fuss and try to follow, dragging her poor legs after her as far as she could. But she seemed to understand that I had to do this myself, and she laid her head down and just watched me go. Malka knew things.

Maybe she was as calm as she was because she knew

where I was headed. We'd been hiding and playing there since we were both little: my mother calls it "Sooz's Forest," and so does my stupid uncle Ambrose, but nobody else would. It's definitely *not* a forest—just a sunny place with mossy trees and noisy birds and a stream too loud for fish. Malka used to hunt rabbits there, and I'd curl up in our favorite clearing and tell myself stories. Sometimes I'd fall asleep in the sunlight and the water's chatter, but she'd always wake me up before dark. And we both knew the way home.

There's a sort of hollow on the far edge of the wood—you have to be looking for it, and you still might not find it—which has always been my particular special place, though I can't ever say why. It's comfortable most of the time, even in winter; and whenever it turned cold, Malka would come and lie down on my chest, and we'd dream. Malka dreamed dog dreams, I guess—anyway, she always twitched a lot. I remember I used to dream about my mother singing lullabies to wolves who were after the sheep . . . except sometimes the wolves were protecting them, and it all would become very confusing. Once I actually dreamed that my brother, Wilfrid, turned into a wolf and flew away, and another time I was a big, ugly bird that kept falling down. And one time . . . but anyway, I always woke up with Malka nuzzling my face, so that was all right. That was home.

But this time it was different. This time it was Jenia.

I didn't know her name then. I thought she was part of another dream . . . and here I'd been trying so hard to stay awake after I whistled Molly's tune exactly—exactly—the way she taught me, right over the griffin's trampled dead body. But today I couldn't get it at all right until I found my way to the hollow. As I've told you, it isn't always there . . . but this time it was, this time I had it just so, and my sister came to me. And there she was, half-hidden in the shadow of a high boulder: too uncertain to be real, but too gray eyed and tumbly haired to be anything else. All my family have eyes like that, even Wilfrid.

"I'm Sooz. Who are you?" I was glad to remember my own name, because I don't always in dreams. I said it again, "Please. I'm Sooz."

She answered me. She told me her name, but I couldn't hear it, even though I saw her lips move. She told me her name for a second time, but I still couldn't make it out. I'd like to think I didn't scream with frustration like a baby, but I probably did. I know me.

Then she was gone, and I was awake and very cold, and I was crying because I wanted Malka. Or my mother, or even stupid Uncle Ambrose . . . somebody who knew who I was, awake or asleep. I don't remember how I got home.

My mother was back from the market by then. She looked straight at me—she didn't know about Molly's promise to me, though I've always thought my father knew something, anyway—and she asked, "What happened? Are you all right?"

I said, "Do I have a sister?"

My mother didn't answer. She just kept looking at me. I asked her again, "I have a sister, don't I? What's her name?"

"I need to call your father," my mother said. She went to the door and called him in from spreading feed for the hogs. I hated the hogs. I hated the sounds they made when they ate, and the sounds they made when they knew they were going to be slaughtered. But there was something in my mother's voice that brought my father to the house in a hurry. He didn't even stop to wash his hands, but stood silently in the doorway, looking first for me, as he always does.

Ever since the time of the griffin, when it started eating children, my father has been different about me, even though that was eight years ago. He can't really go to sleep unless I'm safely in the house, and he'll wake two or three times, most nights, just to be sure I haven't slipped off by myself, the way I did when I went to find the king. My mother puts up with it, but I know it's one reason Wilfrid got married when he did. I don't blame him.

"She knows about Jenia," my mother said. "I thought you ought to be the one to tell her the whole story."

My father is a brave man—a little *too* brave, my

mother thinks—but he turned a bad color just then. He stared at me without saying a word for what must have been a long time, because I can remember the hogs snuffling and quarreling over their meal and the clock ticking and ticking. My mother said, "Ulfi, we can't make her not know. Tell her. Now."

"Sooz," my father said, and then he couldn't say anything for a while. He sat down in the chair that used to be Wilfrid's special chair, and he kept rubbing his eyes, and finally he looked back at me. He said, "Her name . . . her name was Jenia."

"Her name *is* Jenia," I said. "I saw her. That's all I know. Why is that all I know?" A really annoying thought struck me then. "Does Wilfrid know about her?" But I knew the answer before both my parents shook their heads. There was no way in the world that Wilfrid could have resisted crowing to me that he knew something about our family that I didn't.

"She was four years old. Four and a half." My father's voice was clear, but very low, almost a whisper. "Your mother was heavy with Wilfrid then, and it was growing difficult for her to work outside the house, so Jenia was my charge for most of the day. I didn't . . . I didn't mind that much."

He stopped speaking for a little while, and then he went on. "I had to be aware of her every moment—she was so curious, and so *quick*—but she never got herself into any real danger, and she understood the animals. From her first day out of the cradle, she could have fallen into that hog pen right now, at feeding time, and those hogs would have come running to pick her up, and dust her off, and make certain she wasn't hurt. No animal, no one, nothing in the world would have harmed her, from the first. From the first . . ."

His eyes were red rimmed, but he wasn't crying. That's just the way my father's eyes get when he's not letting himself cry. I asked, whispering too now, "What happened to her?"

My mother said, surprisingly sharp, "Let your father tell it. It's his story—I wasn't there." There was a tone in her voice that I couldn't find a word for—not anger, exactly, more a sort of awful tiredness. I had never heard my mother like that.

My father cleared his throat. He began to say, "They took her," but he never got past the first word, and had to start again. He said finally, "They took her. The Dreamies took her. She went with the Dreamies."

The Dreamies . . . the Fae . . . the Others . . . the Good Folk . . . I've heard such names since I was as old as Jenia would have been when she was taken—all the names we have for the shadow people, the ones you only see when they want you to see them, and then just out of the side of your eye. Children see them. I said, "The Dreamies."

"That's what she called them," my father said. "I'd lose

sight of her for a few moments——never more than a moment, I *swear*——and she would always come running back,
laughing, to tell me that she'd been off playing with the
people who came to her in dreams. She said they sang
silly songs and they made her laugh. Once or twice, she
sang one to me."

He kept clearing his throat; it hurt me to hear. I started
to ask about the songs, but he went on. "Children . . .
they make up friends, companions, all the time. Wilfrid
had an imaginary friend named Puddle——you wouldn't
remember that?" I shook my head, and my father almost
smiled. "Wilfrid liked Puddle a lot more than he liked
you, after you were born. It was a long time before he
decided you were even human. But Jenia was . . . gone by
then, and he never. . . ."

He looked far past my mother or me, twisting his fingers hard against each other. I could hear them crack.
"You never told him," I said. "You never told anybody."
My father closed his eyes. I asked, "The Dreamies . . . did
you ever see them? Did they just *take* her? What did
they——?" I stopped, because my father was crying.

He didn't make a sound. He never does. My mother
didn't look away, but I did. Malka pressed against my legs,
whining softly. I'd forgotten she was there. I went to my
father and put my hand on his shoulder, feeling his body
fighting with his breath. My father hates to be out of
control.

"I only saw them that last day. Twilight, it was, and I'd just finished clearing away the new growth of squirrel-weed that keeps sneaking up on the well. You know, once that yellow parasite gets into your water supply, you never get rid of it." He looked around at both of us, as though for agreement. "So I wasn't watching . . . paying proper attention, for that one moment . . . and then I heard her laughing, that way she had. . . ."

For the first time, my mother caught her breath. You couldn't have told it if you hadn't been listening just at that exact moment. My mother is . . . not stronger than my father, not tougher or harder, nothing like that. She just goes somewhere else when she's hurting, while he stays right here. I'm still not sure which of them I'm more like.

My father said, "So I turned, and I was glad, relieved, because I knew I'd let her get out of my sight, and here she was back, the same as always, and *that* was all right, and I'd scoop her up on my shoulders and we'd go up to the house for dinner. And then I saw her. Down in the little wild meadow by the goat path, in the high grass. With them."

His voice didn't change or break; that had already happened, and wouldn't happen ever again. He said, "Small, they were, but not gnomes or elves, none of those folk. They were taller than she . . . than Jenia . . . and they all wore clothes that looked like . . . like *feathers* on them, beautiful *feathers*. And she was so happy to be with them—you could see that even from where I stood. She kept jumping into their arms, and they were swinging her by the hands, up and down . . . the way you always liked us to do, you remember? You used to curl your legs up and *giggle*."

I nodded. My father said, "I called to her. I called until my voice split with it . . . until I fell down to my knees, screaming her name. And she looked back, laughing and waving to me . . . and those others—the Dreamies, or whatever they were—*they* looked at me then, for the first time, and they closed around her straightaway, facing me like a wall of shields—only it was a wall of feathers, you see . . . beautiful, shining, *shining* feathers . . . and in the midst of them, my daughter's joyous laughter as they ran away with her, down toward the river, where I couldn't follow." After a moment, he added, his voice absolutely toneless, "Or wouldn't."

He didn't look at my mother, but I did, and I heard everything they would have said, one to the other, over and over, for seventeen years—my lifetime—until there was nothing left to say, and life still had to be gotten on with. My father said, very quietly, "And so, finally, I had to walk back to the house and tell your mother that our Jenia was gone." He stared straight into my face then, for the first time since he had come home, and added, "There has not been a day, or some part of a day since then, when I have not wished for death."

There was nothing for me to say, so of course I said it anyway, even though I knew what the response had to be. "And you truly never saw her again? Not ever?"

My father shook his head. It was my mother who spoke in that wretchedly silent room, for the first time since she had reproved me for interrupting him. "I dreamed about her for months . . . years . . . so sure she was calling out to me, trying to reach me. I don't dream about her anymore."

"But I *saw* her," I said. "Molly Grue said someone would come to me on my seventeenth birthday, and she did—she came, and she *spoke* to me." I turned from one of them to the other, feeling as young as when I tried to persuade my mother that the big old goat Dithys could talk to me, when he wanted to. "She said her name two times, but I couldn't ever get it, but she was speaking right to me, and I have to go and find her!"

That brought my father to his feet, when I think nothing else could have at that moment. "No, you will *not!*" He shouted the last word, but only that one; everything afterward came out in a cold white monotone. "One daughter gone to those . . . to the Dreamies . . . that is more than enough to lose. I will not risk you—I will not *allow* you. . . ." My mother put her hand on his arm, but he shook it off without noticing. He said, "They took her . . . they shall not have you. If I have to chain you in your room, I will not *let* them. . . ."

When he stopped speaking this time, it felt as though he might never speak again. His body had won out; there was no more breath to be had. My mother said, very gently, "You couldn't keep her from going to seek the king, alone, when she was nine years old." My father did not answer. My mother turned to me. She said only, "Do not go until the lambing season is over. And do not tell him when you go." Then she busied herself in the kitchen, peeling onions.

11

IN FACT, IT WAS WELL PAST LAMBING TIME WHEN I set off in search of my sister. At nine—the age I'd been when I determined to bring King Lír to our village to battle a griffin—other people and their feelings and needs and hurts aren't nearly as real as they become when you're seventeen. Now I knew too much about what losing Jenia had done to my parents, and it was far too easy to imagine what the rest of their days together would be like if I never came back to them. Of course, I was just as certain as that nine-year-old me had been that I *would* be coming home, triumphantly hand in hand with the daughter they had done their best for so many years never to think about or talk about, just as though she had never been born. I fell asleep many a night to that festival in my heart.

Yes, but what if it didn't turn out so? Alone, with no Lír, or Schmendrick, or Molly—or Malka, my Malka, who had never in her life let anything bad happen to me— what if Jenia's terrible feathery Dreamies caught hold of me, and would not ever let either of us go home? *What will I do then?* It's not a nine-year-old's thought, but it was the one I woke up to every morning, no matter how I'd slept. *What could I do?*

Thinking about it now, as honestly as I can, I might have found a really good reason not to go, after all, if Malka hadn't taken the decision out of my hands. She died.

She hadn't been ill—Malka was never ill, not since the day she was born. She was just old . . . but she couldn't have been old enough to die, not *ever*. She couldn't be dead in my bed, with her nose snugged under my arm, the way she always slept, those last years. I held her for a long while—dead for the second time, this time forever—but I didn't cry, not then. That came later, when my mother was holding me. When she said—so softly that I almost didn't hear the words—"You can go now."

It wasn't as simple as that, even so. I buried Malka in Sooz's Forest, where we were happy together, and I came back there most afternoons, just to sit and talk to her. I even sang sometimes, because she always liked that, when I'd make up some silly little song. When I had to leave, I'd say, "Go to sleep now, Malka—go to sleep, good girl. I'll see you in the morning." And so I would, most mornings.

But then my sister came to me again. And this time my father saw her.

He used to come to Malka's grave by himself sometimes. I remember seeing him, standing in the shadows under the trees, not speaking—just watching me being with Malka. I never minded him, never felt that he was intruding on my special time. She was my dog, yes, but we were her family. Malka would have been glad to know he was there.

When Jenia appeared that second time, my father was the one who saw her first. She was kneeling by the stream, showing up more clearly against the wildflowers behind her than she had against the boulder. It looked to me as though she had her hands in the stream, or was trying to, because the water was plainly running through her fingers without touching them. She raised her head then, looking straight at us, and the sadness in her face had me on my feet, calling her name. But my father called to her first.

I don't want to remember his voice then.

He called her "Jeanie." My mother told me later that he was the only person who did.

I don't know whether she heard us or not, but I've always been certain that she saw us. Her hands came up, and she reached out toward us—*for* us, I *saw*—and then she was gone again, without a sound, without leaving a footprint or breaking a twig. My father and I held each other for a long while before either of us spoke.

"I knew she had to be alive," my father whispered. "I didn't . . . sometimes I didn't *want*, I was *afraid*—but I always knew. . . ."

I stared at him. I asked, "Afraid that she'd come back? I don't understand."

My father's answer came word by grinding word. "You didn't see her when she went off with . . . them. She looked so *happy*—so *surely* happy—as though these were the people she belonged with . . . as though she'd been waiting for them all her little life, and they had finally come for her. What if that was really so . . . that we somehow had her by mistake? All these years, and I still lie awake some nights . . . *thinking*. . . ."

I know those stories, about the Fae or the Good Folk, taking a human baby for their own. I said loudly, "*No!* No, I don't believe it! She's yours—*ours*—and she's trying to find her way back to us, and I'm going to get her, and I'll take her away from them, if I have to!" I hadn't been meaning to say all that—it just came out in a single rush—but I guess it had been waiting inside me for longer than I knew. I said, "I *will*! And I'm going tomorrow!"

I hadn't planned to say *that*, either, but none of it mattered anymore. Whatever else she might be, she was real. She was Jenia, my sister.

To my surprise, he didn't argue or fight with me about any of it. Looking back, he must have already gone through all of that with my mother—everything he could have said, and everything I'd have said back, night after night—and by then, the two of us beside Malka's grave, it was already over.

I provisioned myself a bit more practically than when I was nine years old, off in the night to see the king. A blanket, a spare pair of trews, warm stockings (it never crossed my mind to bring those the other time), some dried meat and fruit, and the largest canteen I could comfortably carry. Also, for the first time, I brought a knife. Not a magical sword, or even an elegant princely dagger, it was just my father's second-best sheep-gelding knife, which he used for all manner of things besides making certain that a flock would have only one ram. No larger than one of my mother's knitting needles, it felt cumbersome as an ax in my hands, but it felt good, too. I'd never had a knife of my own before. I didn't ask permission to take it with me. He must have known, though, because we spoke together on the night before I left, and the knife was on my bed, glowing sullenly in the lamplight. My father eyed it, but he never reached to pick it up.

I can remember that farewell talk to this day, word for

word. He sat and watched me finishing my packing, such as it was, constantly closing my knapsack and then deciding to take along a different cooking pot, or choosing sturdier boots over my elegant elkskin pair. Only when I was done did he ask me, "Do you know what I'm most afraid of?"

I turned and waited. My father said, "Not that you won't find her—that she won't come back to us. You're my brave girl, and I do believe you will bring her home safely." He clasped his hands in front of him, knitting the fingers tightly. "But there is an old saying about the Good Folk."

"That you must make sure to call them by that name," I said. "In case they are nearby, and hear you. Yes, I know that."

"No. There is . . . there is an older tale." My father stood up and took hold of my shoulders. He gripped me gently, but I could feel the pain in his hands. He said, "Sooz . . . what the Good Folk take, they replace, always. Steal a boy, give back a boy. Steal a girl . . ."

I could feel my fingertips and the roots of my hair slowly turning cold. I said, "She was gone before Wilfrid was born."

"And then you came to us." My father's hands tightened. "And we couldn't have loved you any more if you . . ." For the first time he looked away from me.

"If I what?" Fear made me suddenly angry. *"If I what?"*

My father licked dry lips, knuckled his mouth. He said, "The oldest story is that the Good Folk steal human children because they have none of their own—they can't *make* children. But they are always very careful to leave a . . . a substitute each time, because if they did not, people would grow alarmed and set out to hunt them down. Do you see, Sooz?"

I saw, but I did not want to see. I said, "But they left no replacement for Jenia."

"No. Perhaps because she went with them willingly, of her own choice—I do not know. They have their own ways and reasons, and their own humor. And then Wilfrid was born, and there were other things to think about. We never forgot our firstborn—never—but we learned to live with her loss, as people do." He released his grip on my shoulders, but his eyes were still pleading for understanding. He said, "Then *you* . . ."

"Then *I* was born." When I was little, I always liked to have my parents tell me, again and again, the story of how I came into the world, came to be with them. I liked it best when my father told it, because he added new details every time—and if I failed to notice the difference in his tone, or how often my mother asked if I wouldn't like to hear a different story, just for a change, it still remained my favorite . . . especially the part where I got to break in to announce, "Then *I* was born!" I never missed the line unless I was well asleep; and even then. . . .

"Sooz," my father said. "Sooz."

I have never been so frightened. I can say that now.

"You were not born to us." I started to pull back from him, to run away, but my father's arms were around me, holding me desperately tightly, almost crushing me. "Sooz, we . . . we found you."

"Found me?" I could only whisper, because my throat felt as though it were bleeding, as though I had swallowed glass. "Found me where? On your doorstep? Isn't that where lost princesses usually fetch up? Maybe I'm an abandoned princess, left with a peasant family." I could see the words hurt him. I meant them to.

But strangely, my father smiled: sadly, yes, but with remembered sweetness as well. "Malka," he said softly. "She was as new as you then. Barely past nursing, she was, must have had her mother all to herself—maybe the other pups had died in the womb, the way it happens sometimes. But Malka was strong and hungry—couldn't walk any more than you could, but already she had her eyes almost open . . . so you would have been the first thing she ever saw." He forced a chuckle, plainly hoping that I would laugh with him. "Because, you see, you were in the basket with her. Sound asleep, you two puppies—never woke up, even when we took you into the house with us. Where you came to live, ever after."

He told it as hopefully as one of his bedtime stories, but clearly seeing the ending in my eyes. It sounded like someone else answering him. I said, "*They* put me in the basket, didn't they? Tucked the little substitute up, safe and warm, with the nice little doggie, then scampered away—exchange accomplished, *that's* done." I was shaking, and I couldn't make words come out right. "They *traded* me. For my sister."

"We never thought of that—never! Sooz, you must, must believe me! We were just so grateful to have you, we never asked questions—never thought about anything beyond the kindness of fate—"

I didn't let him finish. "Well, here's one question perhaps you should have asked. Where did I come from?" His face turned deadly still. I said, "If they can't have children, how did they . . . how did they make me? Am I really a stone? A tree? A fish? A chair, like Wilfrid's chair? A shoe?" I wrenched away, though he continued trying to hold me. "If you love me, tell me what I am! What I truly am!"

He made hushing gestures, nodding toward the door, indicating that he didn't want me to wake my mother. I didn't care. I howled at him, "You know, you know! I don't believe you don't know! Tell me!"

I think for the first and only time in both our lives, my father was afraid of me. I was afraid of myself just then, shaking and stammering with rage as I was. Remembering now, I am astonished that I didn't cry—not once, not at all. I should have cried, surely.

"The Good Folk," my father said quietly, tonelessly. "When they take a child, they leave something in its stead. A cat . . . a pig . . . a log of wood . . ."

"A log of wood," I said. I closed my knapsack for the last time, and stood up from the bed. "There you are. A log of wood—and they even threw in a newborn puppy." I was struggling even then into my own best cloak, while he watched me. "Not a bad bargain, when you think about it."

I still regret not having looked back at him when I walked out of the house where I had lived all my life. I should have looked back. It hurts me still that I didn't turn my head.

He did not follow me. Maybe I expected him to; maybe he expected me to pause on the doorstep and turn. All I remember is that I struck off blindly into the night, past the barn, past the pigpen, where the hogs snorted sleepily to watch me go by; past the huge old walnut tree that Wilfrid and I used to climb together, when he was in a mood to race a baby sister to the highest branch; past the foxes' lair under the overhang, where I had to explain to Malka again and again that she was to leave that particular little family particularly alone. Past the wild grove where Marcos Mamnemos kissed me, and I slapped him. I don't regret that, anyway. He smelled like his father's salt-fish house: half-price, and already half-spoiled, as everyone knew. His son's kisses were just the same.

INEVER STOPPED RUNNING THAT NIGHT. SOME-
times I stumbled into a hurried, blundering walk, knapsack banging between my shoulder blades, but for the most
I just kept lunging along all night, hoping for day to find me
in country where only the Good Folk would recognize a
log of wood shaped into a woman. Which was completely
stupid: my family were well-known among these sheepfolds
and dairies, and it would take me a longer run than that to
stumble among people who did not remember me learning
to walk. I finally had sense enough to sit down on a stone to
get my breath and my bearings.

Where was I bound? It wasn't like being nine years
old, and being lucky enough to have Schmendrick and

Molly Grue take me to meet the king. I had no idea where my sister, Jenia, might be, nor . . . nor *how* she might be, among the people who had stolen her away, if stolen her they had. All I could do was assume that she was aware of my trying to find her, and that she must want to help me—or why would she have shown herself, not only to me but as well to my father? Thinking about him, and the way I had parted from him, made my stomach hurt, so I had to think about something else.

I wondered how she might feel about being rescued by a substitute sister, related to her neither by blood nor by nature. That set me wondering whether a transformed log of wood could ever have a human heart. I put my hand on my own breast, and was almost certain I felt urgent ordinary life stirring there. But I didn't know what that meant anymore.

I finally stopped that and took my father's knife from my knapsack, balancing it on the back of my hand. Considering its single purpose, it was a graceful construction, with a kind of daintiness about it that I had never needed to notice before. I turned it over and over in my hand for a long time in the morning sun. Finally, perched on that stone, I spoke aloud to my sister—to Jenia.

"If you can hear me, help me. I'm going to throw this knife into the air, and from wherever it lands I will walk the road its blade tells me to follow. I'll do this again and again, as long as I must, until I find you. If you hear me, help me now." And I tossed the knife.

It seemed to take forever turning over and over in the air, glittering in the dawn. When it fell to the ground at last—no more than a few feet from my stone—I pounced after it, and discovered the open blade pointing leftward, down a thin, overgrown lane that I'd already overlooked. I looked quickly around me, cleaned the knife against my boot, took a single long breath, and set off down that scratch of a road, brushing aside vines and twiggy branches, until it vanished into a shapeless clearing with no further direction that I could see. But I threw my father's knife once again: this time it alarmed me by bouncing off a tree and becoming briefly lost in a tangle of thorny brush. When I finally found it, the blade was sending me directly back as I had come, to a path that I could only follow by lowering my head like a goat and stubbornly pushing my way through. It took me an hour.

But it didn't matter at all, because I saw my sister again. Jenia.

She came to me this time in twilight, after a day that had taken me through wilder country than the Midwood, which was still my notion of fearsome, even with the griffin long gone. My face was scratched, my clothes were torn, my wrist strained from constantly throwing the knife ahead of myself. I was too exhausted to eat anything; and there had been no further indication that Jenia had as much as a notion that I was seeking her—or would welcome me if she knew. All I could do was what I was doing.

I had made myself as comfortable as I could between the roots of a tree, built the best fire I could—my father never could teach me properly—and was fumbling in my knapsack for a mouthful of dried meat, when she was there, directly across my feeble flames, closer and clearer than I had ever yet seen her and looking straight at me. I remembered the family-gray eyes and the tumbly dark hair most of us have, but I hadn't realized that she was tall, almost my father's height; nor that she was actually beautiful, with near-transparent light brown skin, and the cheekbones of a great cat. I said, "Hello, it's me. It's Sooz." After a moment, I added, "I'm on my way."

She heard me—I was sure of that by now—but she could not speak to me, though she was plainly trying. I said, "Keep leading me, because I don't know where I'm going. But I'll find you. However long it takes, I will find you."

And she smiled at me. Transfigured log or not, I couldn't breathe properly for a moment. It happened like that when I first saw the unicorn, but it was different now. I was different. She stretched a hand out toward me, certainly saying something . . . and then she was gone again, and I curled as close to my limping little fire as I could get, and nibbled my dried meat until I fell asleep. My mouth was painfully dry, but it felt as though I had wakened up smiling. Maybe I had.

I'll never be sure exactly when or where I crossed into the country of the Dreamies. It could have been that same night; it might even have happened without my knowing, while I was storming away from my father, already missing him, log of wood or no. Perhaps all you need to find your way to that other side is truly—*truly*—not to know who or what you are. My sister was barely over four, after all.

All I knew then was that the land I was passing through was growing wilder by the hour, gradually opening out of heavy, smothering woodland into strange shadows of trees and great standing stones, and overhanging hills like massive eyebrows. I recognized nothing, caught quick glimpses of animals I couldn't identify, and was thoroughly lost within a day. But I pushed ahead, still confidently following the guidance of my father's little sheep-gelding knife: sometimes hurling it ahead of me, sometimes spinning it on a bit of flat ground, then trudging along faithfully in the direction the point seemed to indicate—toward my sister. . . .

And all the while . . . all the while, as though they were watching a child playing with sticks and homemade dolls. . . .

I never saw them.

No, that's not true. I did see them, but never as men,

not until it was too late. They were like the shadows of clouds: shapeless and still, stirring only at the whim of the wind, owing allegiance to no particular point of the compass. They made no more sound than the clouds. Even when they were doing what they did to me, they made no sound. I think there were three of them. There could have been four.

No, there were four. That was the one who sang to himself all the time, so softly that I sometimes forget that he was there. But when I dream, I remember him, always. He's always there, with his sad little song.

When they were done, they pulled my clothes back over me—quite carefully, even gently, for all the world as though they were burying me—and then they were gone. And I was gone, too, wandering in my blood and my pain, and my horrible loneliness. I half slept and half woke, half wept; screamed in the darkness—for night had fallen by then—and quickly made myself stop, afraid that those men might return. The moon rose, and it hurt me. I covered my face with both my arms.

And I wanted Molly Grue. Even now, to this day, I have never wanted to see anyone—anyone—as I wanted Molly's sardonic, plain, wonderful face. Not my parents, never my mother and father—*oh, they must never, never. . . .* My mother would hold me, and my father would hire help with the sheep and goats for her, and set out on the silent hunt—my father, who had never raised a hand, let alone a weapon, against another person in his life. But such things, and worse, had been done to Molly in the greenwood when she was younger than I, and she hadn't died . . . no, not died, but survived fully, kind and fearless, to live her life and find her magician—and her unicorn. And so would I, surely . . . surely. . . .

So I lay there under the moon, not crying anymore— nor ever since—and when the bright shadow spilled over me, I was ready to do what I knew Molly would have done. I seized on my father's little knife and I lunged upward with all the strength that hopeless rage had lent me, into the darkness over me. I like to think that I rasped out a challenge of some sort, but memory is most likely flattering me. But what I do recall, and will to my last day, is the tiny gasp of pain that followed my strike, and the terrible sweet ease with which even a farm tool slips through flesh. And may all the gods forgive me, in that moment it felt good—it made my belly happy, and my bones—and I thought, *My family must never know about this, either. Never . . . not ever . . .*

The effort of attacking had brought me to my feet, and I found myself facing a girl—no, a woman—dressed in a peasant's wool smock, colorless with age and wear. She was taller than I—though no older at first glance—longer legged and wider shouldered, with blunt, almost animal features. My father's knife—*my* knife now—was sticking out of her side, a bit below her right breast.

She bent her neck to study the injury, not at all unsteady on her feet; then she casually plucked the knife out of her body and held it flat on her palm for a little moment. Very softly, she said, as though to herself, "I have no luck." She dropped the knife beside me, and touched her hand to the slit in her wool smock, from which it ought to have come away sticky with blood. But all I saw was a trickle of something like dust-colored sand. I thought I could hear the harsh whispering of the grains against each other.

"No blood," I said stupidly. "I mean, good—that's good, no blood—I mean, please, I'm sorry—did I hurt you?" I was babbling from both fear and relief, but I couldn't stop myself. "Please, did I hurt you?"

She shook her head, regarding me calmly out of eyes the color of the strange dust floating from the wound that I had made in her side. "But *you* are hurt—I thought you might be dead yourself, or dying. I came near to see—to help, if I could." Her sudden smile was no more than a wry twitch, but there was amusement in it. "It would seem that you can take excellent care of yourself."

I would have fallen almost at her feet if she had not caught me and held me upright. Her body felt strange against mine: heavy and dense with cold, like the flesh of a serpent, yet somehow not repellent or frightening. I said, "I was sure you were one of them . . . those men. Please forgive me, I'm so sorry." I did not weep—there were no tears left in me, as I've said—but my own body shook with the need of it. I could hardly hear myself saying, "I don't understand."

"How could you? I am sure you have never met anyone like me before." Her voice was low, as deep as a man's. She said, "My name is Dakhoun." That's not all the name she told me, but that's as near to it as I can ever come: as she pronounced it, it is longer than all the gods' names run together, and sounds more like a cough than anything else. I always called her simply Dakhoun.

"I'm Sooz," I said, and surprisingly, she laughed a little. Even her laughter had a slow weight to it: almost a grinding sound. Apparently in her own language, my name is close to the word for a child's toy, something a bit like the cup-and-ball playthings my father used to make for Wilfrid and me. When she spoke my name it came out Sooo-WUZ, every time.

I told her what had happened to me, and apologized again for striking at her. I told her, "Surely . . . see, it's only a small farm knife, my father's knife. . . ." I picked it up and showed it to her on my palm. I told her what it was for. "You see, there's not even any blood. . . . It couldn't really kill anyone." The blade felt strangely warm.

Dakhoun said quietly, "Perhaps it could only kill a laadriak." The word seemed to tear its way out of her mouth, snagging on her lips and teeth. "Perhaps that was its true purpose."

"Laadriak." In the feeble dawn she continued to appear close to my own age. Her skin was the golden brown of desert honey, but her eyes and hair were oddly pale, almost the shade of running water. I asked, "Are they your people, the laadriak?"

Dakhoun laughed again, but not at all in the way that she'd laughed at my name. "The tribe to whom I was born call themselves the Kadri. *Laadriak* is the word that the Kadri have for people—beings—like me. The ones made of stone."

The gray dust was still drifting from the wound below her breast. I remembered her hard heaviness in my arms. I said idiotically, "Stone. The laadriaki . . ." I shook my head, trying to keep from gaping at her.

Dakhoun said, "From time to rare time among my tribe, a child is born who is not . . . not of human flesh. Custom decrees that such a monster must be immediately destroyed, and never spoken of again. And it is surely right that this should be so."

There was a slight questioning lilt in the last words, as though she might be expecting agreement. I said nothing, and after a moment Dakhoun went on. "Yet my parents loved me from my first breath, and took it upon themselves to raise and shelter me like anyone else's child." Her voice seemed to issue from a bottomless well of weariness and loss. "Had they not been of high standing among the Kadri, I would not be here now. Even so, the fear and anger against them grew so great over the years that one night, for their sake, I slipped away and set out alone into the world." The pale eyes had grown dark with memory; yet again there came that sudden strange twist of a smile. "To seek my fortune, as the old tales will have it."

"Stone," I said again. "Yet I . . . but the knife—I mean the knife, it went . . ." I couldn't bring myself to say the rest; instead I blurted, "How can you be of . . . of stone, then?"

Dakhoun shrugged: an oddly slow and even awkward movement in her tall body. "As much as the Kadri ever speak of us, it is said that all laadriaki have a single vulnerable place—otherwise we would master the entire tribe, and rule forever." After a moment, she added without expression, "When I was small, it was the great delight of other children to seek out my weak spot. It was, you could say, a favorite sport."

Remembering games that my brother Wilfrid and my cousins had invented to play with me unobserved brought a shortness to my breath, and a thickness to my words. "I cannot tell you. . . ."

The gesture that silenced me was impatient, but somehow kindly. "Please, never tell me again that you are sorry for trying to kill me. Trust me when I say that I am far more grateful than you can be grieved. It is lonely being what I am—one of a scattered handful of laadriaki ever to survive past birth, and my mother and father. . . ."

Here she paused briefly, looking past me. "My parents did me ill service, keeping me alive as they did. I am duty bound to remedy their error, that is all. But I must certainly tend to you before I continue on my search. If you will allow me . . ."

I never heard her speak her own tongue, the language of the Kadri, so I've no notion whether it was as formal and dryly distancing a sound as she made of ours. I protested weakly—how faraway my modesty seems to me now, after where those four men had taken my body and my spirit—but it was comforting all the same to allow another woman to hold me, to cleanse me, as best she could, of what had been done to me . . . to someone else . . . somewhere terribly else. . . .

I don't know how long I slept while she was setting about me: washing me with her own drinking water, soothing my bruises with soft cloth, most likely torn from her own garments. I woke only when she had let me lie back in the tangled grasses, and was standing herself, turning away, hoisting the small traveling bag I had not noticed until then. She looked pale, and very tired.

I scrambled to my feet, startling her. "Where are you going?" Then, remembering the last thing she had said, "What are you seeking? Perhaps I . . . could I help?" In that moment, the thought of being abandoned to my own memory was suddenly more than my loneliness could bear.

8

When she turned back to look at me, the silence of her eyes made me believe that she might truly be made of stone. She said, "I am looking for Uncle Death. I believe I would have found him in the night had I not turned aside for you. But I will overtake him today—tomorrow, at the latest. He will wait. He told me so."

"Oh," I said. We looked at each other. "I'm looking for my sister. She went away with the Dreamies—the Good Folk—when she was little, and now I'm trying to find her. But I got *lost*. . . ." And suddenly I couldn't speak any further. But I was not crying. I was *not*.

Dakhoun came closer. She dropped her bag, without seeming to notice. "How long ago did you lose your sister? Ten years—fifteen—"

"Twenty . . . I wasn't born—"

"And you cannot say whether she is still alive—?"

"Yes, I can!" In that moment I was simply an indignant child. "She has come to me three times, and every time she's made it very clear that she wants me to find her where she is and bring her home to our father and mother." After a moment I corrected myself. "To our parents." Even as short a time as I'd known her, I did not think for a moment that she missed the change.

"Twenty years . . ." Dakhoun seemed to be addressing someone else; certainly not me. "Well. And here I am, still following Uncle Death's trail for longer than that,

104

and never yet a proper sight of him. We are well met, after all."

Longer than that. . . . How old was she, then? All I knew in the world at that moment was that I did not want her to leave me. I said, "So here we are——a stone woman looking for Death, who plainly keeps slipping away from her"——Dakhoun bridled, but did not deny me——"and a transformed log seeking her sister. Oh, well met, indeed."

It says something for Dakhoun that she did not immediately inquire as to what I could mean by referring to myself as a transformed log. What matters is that she laughed outright for the first time. It might have leaped out of an utterly different throat, so true and warm and purely delighted a music it was. It wrapped me in safety for a small moment, that laughter, and I hear it still.

"Why not? Indeed, why not? After all, one should always have company on the road to Uncle Death, and you and I may actually be quite suited, when we consider the matter." She peered sharply down at me, as though she were perched on a higher branch than I had realized. She said, "But when he does turn to face me——finally——you must step aside and never look back. We have unfinished business between us."

"Agreed," I said. "And when I find my Jenia——and I will——and take her away from those who stole her, we will be going home together straightaway." Perhaps it was the echo of her laughter that made me add, "If I can ever find the way." And we laughed together for the first time.

"Well," she said. "If you feel able to walk. Death said he would wait for me, but not forever."

And so we set off together, Dakhoun and I.

IV

SHE HAD NO MORE NOTION OF WHERE DEATH might be sought out—for all her assurance, I realized that during our very first day on the road—than I had of where to look for my sister. Jenia had not shown herself since . . . since those men . . . and I couldn't stop myself from thinking that there must be some connection between what had happened and her absence. I kept wheeling around and staring in every direction as we tramped along, trying to wish that shadow, that silent voice, into existence, if only I could stare and wish hard enough. But any whisper of her echoed inside me, nowhere else, and there was nothing at all to do but blunder on through the country of the Dreamies.

The country of the Dreamies . . .

Even now, at times, I think there is no such place, that I talked myself into believing—dreaming, even—that landscape, constantly changing: desert dissolving to marsh to sudden spring meadow, flowing into farmland too sadly like my home, to melting into dark evergreen forest. All of it magical and unreal as any dreamland . . . and more unreal because I could touch a leaf, or feel an insect crawling across my hand. And if that makes no sense, I can't help it.

Sometimes I almost convince myself that every bit of it was set up, planned out for me, all for my benefit, like one of those hero plays that traveling troupes used to put on in the marketplace. But most often I still think they were making it up as they went along, day to day, moment by moment, the way children do. Children make up the world as they need it, day by day.

But I saw no children in the country of the Dreamies. Not one.

Beyond being possessed by finding my sister, I didn't want to see anyone in those earliest days in that strange, strange place. I was always seeing those four men, seeing them seeing me, those four, wherever I turned my head, staring at me out of all shadows, peering up from the bottom of the streambeds Dakhoun and I waded across, looking down from treetops, clouds, great boulders—the way I saw Jenia for the first time in my life. Seeing me . . .

The Dreamies saw me, too.

I only began to glimpse them after I met Dakhoun—if *met*'s the right word for trying to kill a stranger. Before then, wandering alone, I'd seen squirrels, birds, little blue snakes with tiny hands, sheep and goats, such as my family raised—even a couple of creatures I can't name to this day. No, I can, but I don't want to. But the Dreamies, the ones who took my sister, they were no more than occasional murmurs, glimpses, midnight whispers, even when I knew what they must be. Dakhoun would sometimes nudge me, usually not looking at me, pointing off toward rustling, shining shadows that were too quick for me to recognize at first.

But the faces, when they came clear . . .

Oh, those lovely, lost, wise, half-mad, sweetly evil faces of the Dreamies, peering back at me out of bushes, thickets, even pools—those faces suddenly next to mine for a moment—prancing in the trees, swimming down the moonlight. They teased me awake with giggles and soft chuckling; they spoke to me, and I almost understood.

Most often they came a little before dawn, or just beyond sunset. They didn't all look alike: it took me some while to recognize individuals—the cackling, sneering witchy woman; the limping near-bear who seemed to come and go like a candle flame; the woman who always seemed to be stalking silently between Dakhoun and me; then the dark-eyed, laughing, monkey-browed girl; the sweet-faced man like an elderly angel. . . . Were these the same ones who had taken her? The ones who had lured her from us when she was too little to know what they were? "The Dreamies," she called them, my father said, because they came to her in her sleep. "They sang silly songs and they made her laugh. . . ."

They didn't sing to me. Between their taunting bright-ness and the hands and the smells of those four men, I slept poorly in the country of the Dreamies. But I saw them, and they saw me . . . they saw me, just as my sister had, never a doubt of that, and each one of those faces gaily threatening me, warning me to abandon my search and find my way back to the world I belonged to, for worse things than what had yet happened to me were waiting just beyond the very next twist in the road. Or the river—for there was one now and then, twinkling beside us in proper fairy-tale style, before it wandered off toward those low hills or that tangly wood, while we kept slogging more or less eastward. Even the sun and stars couldn't be trusted in that country—I lost time there as quickly as I lost direction.

I looked for them constantly, the faces of the Dreamies. I looked into them eagerly, greedily, one after another, as they showed themselves, trying to find some way behind that brightness, into whatever charm could have drawn my Jenia so happily away from the family who cherished her so. But they laughed and played with me, and told me nothing, the faces, and there was nothing to do but trudge on, side by side with the woman I had tried so hard to kill.

She was a troublesome traveling companion in certain ways, Dakhoun, until I became accustomed to her habits and her manners. She set a sturdy pace, striding out ahead of me on those long legs, and I often had to scurry to keep up. Yet from time to time, she would abruptly turn from the trail—such as it was, in whichever brand-new land-scape the Dreamies had invented for us overnight—and actually leap to this side or that, sometimes to be gone for nearly half an hour, while I stumbled on. When I asked her the purpose of this, she replied shortly, "He is cunning. He plays silly tricks." Seeking Death she might be, but she never had any great respect for him.

Made of stone or not—and my only evidence of this so far was the cold weight of her body, and the fact that the wound that I had made below her breast never quite closed—she was certainly stronger than anyone I'd ever known. Just how strong I learned when we were crossing a turbulent river on a footbridge—as I've said, the country seemed to change its shape and texture daily— and I fell through a gap in the vines. Dakhoun snatched me from the grip of the air almost before I realized that I was falling, and hauled me to solid ground by one ankle, which bore the mark and bruise of her grip for days after-ward. She was not even breathing hard as she turned me right side up and set me on my feet.

When, breathless enough for both of us, I thanked her for saving my life, she looked startled, as though she had done it in her sleep, and had only now become aware of the act. She replied in the mock half grumble, which was increasingly our most truthful means of communication, "Mind those great feet, girl! I cannot be forever rescuing you from all those plots and traps they lay for you." I laughed, which was her intent, and we crossed the footbridge together in safety.

Food was chancy at the best of times, which concerned Dakhoun not at all. "Why should stone eat? It was always a trouble to my poor mother that I would never nurse, and only ate once in a while, to please her. But what should stone do?" She lived on rainwater, as far as I ever knew; sometimes, rarely, she nibbled a roadside weed that looked like broomstraw. "It has no taste, none, but it is quite nourishing. If you have to eat."

Yet, to my surprise, she turned out to be a remarkably efficient hunter. The only trouble was that our meals— my meals, really—turned up at odd hours; most often toward dawn or twilight, but frequently in cold midnight, when she would wake me to insist on my dining immediately. Which meant that almost everything I ate—root, rabbit, or fish—went down uncooked, which she considered by far the healthiest manner. In her own way, she was doing her best for me.

She wasn't much for conversation. We often went entire days with nothing between *good morning* and *good night*, except perhaps *watch out* at a pit or a deadfall. I think that at times she surely must have regretted allowing me to attach myself to her quest, which was easy for me to understand. Even at my age, it seemed obvious that a serious search for Death had to be a private matter, and I could only pray that when we did come to that turn and finally find Death waiting to keep his long-promised appointment with Dakhoun, I would know to step back and let her go on by herself. I wondered whether or not I should simply say "Farewell, friend" when the moment arrived. I went back and forth with that a good deal, in the night.

She was silently afraid of my father's little knife, though I hadn't yet seen any indication of her failing, not any sign of pain in her pale eyes, or in her bearing. The knife, indeed, looked a deal worse off, showing a blunted tip and a badly gouged blade, looking as though it had been through a fire. As lost as I had been almost since the night I left home, I'd long since given up on imagining it some sort of magical compass; now it simply made me uneasy, reminding me of the moment when it proved useless to protect me. I would surely have rid myself of it, had Dakhoun permitted this. But she never would.

"No, it is not a hero's flaming sword," she said often, "nor is it some hedge wizard's sly staff of wisdom. But something in it was meant for you. Something . . . somehow . . ."

One night, watching me tear open a fat marsh rat—at least, after almost two days of going hungry, it *looked* like a marsh rat—she said thoughtfully, "It is Durli make, did you know that? That means that it was quarried on the Durli Hills by certain smiths schooled to add a certain ore to the mix at a certain moment. I have never seen it used to forge a blade as small as this." She turned the blade on her palm, treating it as always with a respect that I'd stopped according it long since. She said, "It is well made," and nothing more.

She slept seldom, and never completely. A turn in the night by something on a high branch would have her instantly on her feet. Most often, she was the one who woke me out of the dreams that brought me up unable to breathe, striking wildly with my useless knife at the whispers and chuckles in the darkness. She would hold me then—unspeaking herself, always—until I realized once again that the hands on me were hers.

V

I WAS THE ONE TO SEE THE BOY WHEN HE CAME, the first time.

We'd both been seeing the footprints for some mornings, circling us from every angle—dainty and precise, and almost human, except for having four toes on each, divided down the middle, like hoofs, two and two. They had a swagger about them; indeed, a number of the prints had passed impudently close to our sleeping heads, never rousing either of us. Dakhoun shook her fist at those, and swore in her own tongue. After that, she did not sleep at all for some while.

That same day was also the first time that she faltered on the trail. Except for the sand-seeping wound that never closed, just below her heart, I'd almost allowed myself to believe that she was neither in danger nor in pain from my blind, frantic attempt on her life. Seeing those strong legs stumble over a fallen log wasn't what caught my conscience—it was the swift side-glance she stole at me to see whether I had noticed. The weakness never recurred, not then; if anything she increased our pace, and by now I knew her better than to suggest slackening it, or even resting briefly. But there was no disguising my knowledge, or my fear.

That night, sitting across the fire from me in a vine-shrouded clearing, she said, out of a faraway silence, "It is plain that we are never going to find your sister. You should go home."

Until I opened my mouth to answer her, I had no notion of how deep my weariness ran, nor of how deeply it had bitten into my heart since that man who sang to himself had first laid his hands on me. "Where is home?" I asked her. "I've no more chance of finding my way back there than you have of finding Death waiting for you, as he promised." That had been a joke between us once; now it had come as true as breath. All my quest for Jenia had brought me was rape and loss and exile; as for her own mission . . . well, Death had lied to her, as to so many, and that was all there was to that. I said, "I am responsible for you. I will turn back when you do, not a moment before."

She stared at me. I fully expected laughter, a snort of

mockery for claiming any sort of share in her fate. But she only sat staring, as though she had never seen me before, never hunted to feed me, nor ever kept me from tumbling straight down into a wild river. Her winter-pale eyes held me just as fast as her fierce grip had done, and I saw the stone then: the stone skeleton behind the slow-beating heart and the dusty blood still sifting from the wound that I had made. And I saw the parents who had chanced loving her, and because of whom—I've never doubted it— she had turned aside for a ravaged child. For I was a child to her, however few years might lie between us. I saw that then, in those eyes.

She was still sitting by the fire when I finally slept. I don't remember lying down, but I woke so, under her cloak, itself more ragged every day, and ever damp with the morning mist. Dakhoun was nowhere to be seen, but seated almost exactly in her place was a boy who appeared no more than eight or nine years old—the first child I had ever seen in the country of the Dreamies. He was fish pale, with eyes and hair the color of icy slush, and he was leaning toward me, studying me intensely, with his elbows resting on his knees. No, *resting* is absolutely the wrong word for that child: he appeared able to spring to his feet and be gone instantly, leaving behind no memory of his having been there. When he saw that I was awake, he smiled at me with small, sharp fish teeth, and I said, "If you're Death, Dakhoun is looking for you."

The fish teeth showed themselves a bit more, the tips glistening wetly. I was too tired and cold to be afraid of him. I said, "I am sure she will return in a little while. Wait for her."

His voice was lower than I'd have expected, and too sweet. "She's no concern of ours, poor stone thing. You're the one interests us, trailing a sister you've never known through a land that hates you harder than you can imagine, and will make sure you die stupidly lost here, without ever touching her, holding her. And still you keep coming. . . ." He shook his head in mock wonder. "Branded and burned as you are, still you will keep coming forever . . . forever. . . ." The last word sounded like a bell buoy in a rising storm.

"What else should I do?" I asked it in the same way that Dakhoun would ask, "What should stone do?" about her mother's concern that she never ate. I said, "I am not going home without my sister."

"Then you will never go home." The little boy's smile—if he was even a boy—dug hard into my skin. Dakhoun smiled just the same way, but that hurt was different. It always made me want to comfort her, but of course I never did.

"Why did you take her?" I didn't know I was going to ask that until I heard myself. I said, "She was a child—a baby still. You stole her, and you left. . . ."

I thought I could finish it. I tried a second time.

The boy said, "She belonged to us before she was born. We knew she was coming."

I can't say now how I might have answered him, because at that moment he looked up sharply and was instantly gone, just as I had imagined. Dakhoun stood where he had been, carrying by the neck a thing like a sort of fluffy frog with useless bat wings. She had plucked most of the feathers, if that's what they were.

I said, "There was somebody, but I don't think he was Death. I told him you were seeking him, anyway."

"He cannot have been Uncle Death," Dakhoun said firmly. "Uncle Death is a deceiver—always, yes—but he would have waited." She held the frog thing out to me, and there was nothing much I could do as she stood there but thank her and half pretend to be half roasting it in the ashes of our cold fire. She said, "I meant what I told you. If you turn around now and walk away from this place— walk straight back, exactly the way you came, now—this place will let you go, even guide you home to your family. I know this, Sooz." She almost never called me by my name, and she never once got it right.

"When you do," I said, and no more. She shrugged and waited silently until I had done the best I could with the frog thing, choking it down, so as not to insult her foraging. Then we started off, though it was still dark. Day and night were coming to make less and less difference to either of us; Dakhoun seemed to know when I needed rest before I was ready to admit it. We moved on.

The country was changing once again in the dimness—we could actually see it becoming rolling blue-green meadowland almost under our feet. Manageable to walk, and even springy—the turf was alight with bright little purple daisies—but no sign of real road or trail, and almost no trees, so hardly any Dreamies that I noticed. Dreamies like trees. They constantly peer from behind them; they travel in them as easily and naturally as squirrels; sometimes you can actually see them dancing in the highest branches, making faces, singing those silly songs that they sang to my sister in her sleep. Those songs I'll never forget.

I saw the fish-smiling boy—*stupidly lost here*—following us, well away in the dimness, but I pretended I hadn't. *Branded and burned* . . .

I never learned his name. The Dreamies don't have names—I mean, I don't think they do. The ones I came to recognize I more or less thought of as Cat-Rabbit . . . One-eyed Growler . . . Blanket Thief. . . .

I wondered what they called each other. I wondered if they had a special name for my sister.

As though she had been following my thoughts, Dakhoun abruptly asked me, "Do you suppose she will still remember her own name? In this world?"

She had asked the question before. I never had an

answer, so it made me angry. I said, "She knows who she is. And she knows me, and she's not hiding from me, the way Death hides from you." It was as cruel as I meant it to be, and I think sometimes that it hurt her more than my father's little knife ever had done. I apologized before sunrise, and she forgave me sooner than I did. In some ways, I never have.

But she found Jenia when I couldn't. She found her that same day.

It happened late, near dusk, which is when the Dreamies are usually most active. They took Jenia then . . . *no*, they didn't take her, kidnap her—she went off with them happily, eagerly. I had to keep remembering that, seeing my father's eyes when he told me.

Dakhoun and I had stopped for the night in a shallow hollow, crowded with dank dead leaves. Seasons are just as meaningless as time or landscape in that country: you can lie down to sleep on a bland summer evening, and be awakened by snow falling on your face, or by the wailing of a midwinter storm. I lay staring up at the usual empty night sky, wishing to see a single star, or a reassurance of moonlight. But I saw no more stars in the Dreamies' country than I had seen children, and the moon was down.

I must have slept a little, because suddenly I was bang awake and sitting up, and Dakhoun was leaning over me, her pale eyes more intensely triumphant than I'd ever seen them. "*There!*" Her voice, low as it was, crackled like fire in my ears. "*There*, do you see her?" She dragged me to my feet with one hand tight on my arm, and pointed straight into the darkness with the other. "Take her home now, tonight—*go*, the two of you! You go *home!*"

For a moment there was nothing beyond dark: only trees and the gnarly shadows of trees. Only the strange soft pattering that went on all night, every night—the breathing of the Dreamies as they turned in their own restless sleep. At least, that was what I usually imagined it must be: I still didn't know if the Dreamies actually slept, any more than I was ever really sure of much about Dakhoun. All I knew, finally, still half-asleep, but completely clear inside, was that I was never going to find my sister, Jenia; never ever going home. Just then, I was finally too weary to care.

And then I saw her.

And she saw me. She was standing alone on the other side of a shallow stream that had been traveling along with us—except when it wasn't—for some while now. She wasn't wearing those beautiful, frightening feather clothes that my father remembered—I hadn't yet seen any of the Dreamies in anything like that—but in an ordinary sort of gray shift, such as my mother might have worn late in the evening, after a long day's work. Her feet were bare . . . no, those were slippers of some kind, glimmering faintly with their own twilight, like that other strange glint at her throat, almost hidden by her hair. It might have been a pendant, a collar, even a necklace—I didn't know then.

And it didn't matter. I ran to her, splashing across that drowsy little stream, and I grabbed her as hard as I could to keep her from disappearing, the way she'd done before I was born, and every time since. I held on to her, and I kept saying her name, as though I were afraid that one of us might forget it. She went rigid against me for a moment, pulling away—then her arms went around me, and she held me closer than anyone ever had in my life. Including Molly Grue or King Lír. Including my mother and my father. Anyone ever, even now.

"You're Jenia!" I said it over and over. "You're Jenia!"

Because Dakhoun really did have me worried that she might not remember herself, or remember her true name. But she only laughed, and she held me even tighter, until I could barely breathe, and that didn't matter, either. I whispered, "I'm Sooz," even though I knew she already knew my name. "I found you. . . ."

"Yes," she said. "Oh, yes—yes, you did." She caught her own breath, as though it was something she had to chase down. She said, "Yes, you did, my beautiful little sister. And now you have to turn around and leave me, and forget." Her voice was low and shaky, but very clear—almost too clear, somehow. "Tell them . . . tell them you never saw me, that you hunted everywhere, but you never could find me." She tipped my head back gently, and she smiled into my eyes. "Oh, Sooz, they will be so happy to have you home. They'll not ask you any questions, I promise you that."

It took me a moment—no, more than a moment, how could she be saying that?—to find the words to answer her. "No. No, Jenia, I came for you. I came to get you, to bring you back with me." How could she not understand me? Nothing made sense in all this starless, childless land, except knowing that my sister—the end of the journey, the tune I'd whistled over and over to learn (oh, Molly!), the reward and comfort for everything, everything—was here, here with me, rescued at last, coming home after an impossible lifetime of exile.

How could it all not be so?

VI

N o," I said again, as though she had simply misheard. But she was already slipping away
from me, already gone out of my arms, no matter how
desperately I clawed at her plain gray dress to keep her
close. "Don't go! They can't keep you—I'll never let
them!" The sky was spinning; my head and my ears were
racked with my own wailing faraway voice, and I was
sure I was going to throw up. Only the dear lying gods
will ever know everything I promised my lost sister then.

But the Dreamies were already dancing between us,
cackling and crooning, *"Don't go. . . . Oh, my Jenia, don't
ever leave again!"* Barring my way to her, so by the time I
had knocked all the hungry visions aside, she had long
since vanished under mocking noise and laughter. I could

only stand where I was, shaking and helpless. She might never have been there.

At my shoulder, Dakhoun said calmly, "Sooz. It is time to go home."

Would I have responded any differently if she had put it some other way? If she had looked directly at me, shrugged, and simply said, "You heard her." Or said nothing at all, but only raised her eyebrows, in that way she had. No, I don't really think so, even now . . . but maybe I could have said something like, "I don't think so. You go on where you need to go, take care. . . ." And I'd have gone straight after Jenia, without another glance at her, and that would have been the end of it. I'd likely never have seen her again, ever. I've thought about that often.

But what actually happened was that I answered her, "Not a chance. Not a chance in the world." And without looking at her again, I went on where that little stream was going, where she had gone, pushing through the jeering Dreamies—the near-human faces, the faces that weren't the least bit human, and the bodies, the bodies that were growing so beautiful I couldn't bear to look at them, so I didn't. I just lowered my head and kept pushing on.

I didn't think at all about Dakhoun still following me, not until I heard her say sharply, "My friend. Stop now. Please." I kept walking. In a softer voice, she said, "You owe me that much kindness."

Maybe it was that word, *kindness*. I couldn't remember

ever hearing her use the word, not once. It stopped me where I stood, and I turned to look at her.

I don't know if anyone else would have seen what I saw in her pale eyes. I don't think so. Anyone else might most likely have recognized the tireless rhythm of her stride, the patience with which she waited for me to catch my breath or regain my strength; even the way she went prowling every night, bringing me things to eat that I couldn't always identify.

But when I think of it, all I ever see is the lost, elusive wildness in her eyes, a wildness that I have never yet seen in any other. It was always gone in a moment; but for that little time, she might have been a complete stranger: no matter how hard or how deeply I stared at her, not even when I blinked and actually shook my head. But I knew that nameless stranger each time I saw her coming and going. I waited for her.

She said, "Once, some while ago, you announced that you felt . . . responsible for me—that you would not turn back until I did. Do you remember?" I nodded. Dakhoun went on, more slowly: "It took me longer than you will know to admit that I was coming to feel similarly. I have traveled alone for all my life, since I learned what I was. Except for my mother and father, I have never had a friend." She made a try at laughter. "You will have to ex-cuse me, I am not even sure if I could tell you what a friend looks like, or what they do. But I think you might be my one friend, if that should suit you." She looked away for a moment; whether shyly or regretfully, I could not have said. Then her eyes returned to me. "If that suits you."

She was there again, that stranger I could not recognize, any more than I can ever recognize an old song in my sleep. Her eyes were at once fierce and lonely, hungry for something she could not name, no more than I could find a name for her. What I saw then was simply a tall, tired woman, still hunting Death but right now more than willing to settle for company. And whatever I knew, so was I.

She put out her hand to me, only a little hesitantly. The only times she ever did that was either to save my life or to hold me when I was wandering alone through some nightmare. There was nothing for me to do but to take her hand in both of mine and say, as awkwardly as she, "Of course. Of course you are my friend."

She smiled. That, all by itself, was such a slow, rare thing to see that I could not help asking, "Who else?" And we both laughed, looking at each other.

"Well, then," she said. "I will go where you go, but if you are determined to follow Jenia wherever *she* is bound, then you will never catch up with her." After a moment, she added, "As you know."

"It's all I know to do," I said. "And I'm not going home without her. The Dreamies know that."

Dakhoun nodded. "So do I. But there is another way,

if you will allow me." I stared, and she repeated, thinking I'd misheard her. "If you will allow me?"

"Oh." I went on blinking stupidly. "Another way. Yes, certainly. I didn't think. Show me?"

And I was grateful, in honesty, because I knew only to follow that little stream to find Jenia—if, indeed, that was where she had truly gone. Beyond that, I had no further notion of which way to turn for her than I'd ever had. I said, "Thank you. It's good to have a friend."

To my surprise Dakhoun beckoned briskly, starting promptly back almost the way we had come. It made no sense that I could see: the road bent away out of my sight, away from the stream I had scrambled across to reach my sister at last. I protested loudly; but without looking back Dakhoun put her finger to her lips and shook her head, ignoring the assorted Dreamies who kept fluttering derisively after us. It took me too long to realize that the road was bending further, more or less paralleling the stream after all, though it never quite kept the water in sight. But if I stood still, I could just hear it talking to itself, the way water does. I said, "*Oh*. Yes."

"I have no idea whether we will ever come up with your sister. Or when. But we know where she was heading—that much, at least, I am almost sure of." She sighed and squared her shoulders against the burden of her traveling bag. "So. Onward, then?" That had never been a question before.

And on we went, through that unchanging, mindlessly changing land. I only slowly came to understand—as Dakhoun must have known almost on our first day of travel together—that "Dreamie" doesn't only mean the ones who live there, the creatures who stole away my sister . . . my Jenia, as I'd been calling her before I ever met her. It means *that place*, that child's imagining of a world where if you don't want something to stay *this* way or *that* way, you yourself can make it be different. There are no rules, not ever. Children hate rules—except just for a moment, when they need a new game right away. I know. I'm like that myself—or I would be, except for Malka. Malka's rules were always mine.

In a way, then, there *isn't* any world of the Dreamies. There's only now. Endless *now*.

We kept going, my stone companion and I. Every now and then, I found myself slowing down, or even stopping, because there'd be a couple of Dreamies I'd never seen before: two half bears chasing each other through the underbrush; I still don't know what the other half really was. A group of what looked for a tantalizing moment to be children, snarling and blocking our way until we were nearly on them, and then turning into little tree frogs as they went dancing away.

I'd gape for a moment, forgetting where I was, almost wishing they could stop their everlasting game and talk to me. Because, except for that strange boy with his glinting too-sharp fish teeth, crouched by my dying fire in the morning, I'd never spoken a word to even one Dreamie in all the days I'd been wandering through their country. The truth is that I never really got over being afraid of them. I can admit that now. Part of it is that they were all forever mixed-up in my head with those men who lived there and still do—still do, still do, and only Dakhoun can ever know.

One chill night I woke, not from a nightmare but to a question which brought me awake and staring, as it would for many nights to come. What if she wanted to come home with me—I fell asleep so often dreaming of just that—but for some reason she *couldn't*? Suddenly I'd be wide-awake, thinking, *Suppose she really wants to come away with me, but she can't pass out of this place, can't pass the entrance, no matter how hard she tries. What then? What will I do then?*

I remembered that boy warning me, "She belonged to us before she was born. . . ." What did that mean? When did my sister, Jenia, and I—separately, years apart— really pass into the country of the Dreamies? Where did we actually cross the line? Would I know? Would I trust any of these creatures to tell me?

Dakhoun . . . Dakhoun told me once, but I wasn't listening. If I turned around and walked straight back, exactly the way I'd come, then I'd be home before the Dreamies could ever stop me. How long ago that all seemed . . . before those men hurt me, before Dakhoun herself. When I questioned her about that, as we trudged on, her shrug was barely visible. "Why ask me? You are bound and determined to follow her, as I am absurdly determined to accompany you, though neither of us has more than a guess at where we might be going. What does it matter now?"

"I don't have a choice—I've told you that!" She didn't even bother shrugging this time. We didn't talk for a long while after that.

I caught sight of Jenia twice, that same afternoon. The first time, she was surrounded by what looked like a whole glowing cluster of fireflies, sparking on and off, even in her hair. But if you stared long enough, they melted into flights of sweet little bugs . . . only they weren't such sweet little bugs when you looked really closely at them. The second time, she was just walking on the very far side of the stream by herself. I would have gone straight to her then—she seemed so very much alone, with no Dreamies crowding and pushing at her. But Dakhoun touched my wrist silently, and I saw three or four creatures flanking her at a little distance. They were bigger than the usual run of Dreamies, not much but enough to be noticed, and for the first time I saw them in the glowing feathers my father had told me about. I don't exactly know how to talk about them, except to say that they were all almost beautiful, but not quite. I *think*

I mean that in the way they came and went; they hurt your eyes, just a bit, they shivered between *here* and *there* just a bit, between *gone* and *back* and *almost*, just so. They felt dangerously lovely, but you could never ever get a proper fix on them, because they'd never stay entirely still . . . never entirely. And that's the best I can do, and I know it's not right.

Even so, I would have run to her anyway, but for the look on Dakhoun's face. I whispered "What? *What?*" Because I needed so much to hold my sister again, my legs were trembling.

Dakhoun said, very low and clear, "If you do what you want, she will vanish, and this time you will never see her again." I remember, I was still half-crouched to run when she said that. She went on, cool as always: "Right now, she thinks you have taken her warning—given up, gone home. She will not make that mistake ever again, and she knows how to hide in this place far, far better than you will know. Keep out of sight, and keep on. Do it, Sooz."

She didn't raise her voice at all, but it was only the third time since I'd known her that she called me by my name. We kept walking. In a moment, Jenia had passed from view again—there was a dip in the road, and then a flurry of things like flying flowers hiding her altogether. We didn't see her all the rest of that day.

That night we scooped water from the stream, and didn't bother with an evening meal. Dakhoun politely offered to go hunting, as usual, but I was too tired and sad even to think about being hungry. I made a fire—something the Dreamies never needed to do, I'd noticed—while Dakhoun sat watching me, never once taking her eyes from me, which always made me nervous. Strange, when you think about it: this stone friend, who had healed and comforted me, who had fed and protected me from all dangers, never ceased to mystify and puzzle and sometimes frighten me. And the wound that I had made in her side never quite closed.

I spoke wearily at last. "Do you suppose . . . tomorrow?"

Dakhoun did the thing with her shoulders I had decided must be a shrug. "Tomorrow, the next day, I cannot tell you. Sooner or last . . . yes, we will catch up with her sooner or later. And then you will have one chance—one chance alone, do you hear?—to persuade her to come away, to come home with you." She turned from me and lay down. "How you will do that is altogether up to you."

I said nothing. After a long time, long after I thought she was asleep: "If I might say one more thing . . ." I didn't answer. Dakhoun said, "Do not run and pounce on her. She will be gone like *that*—" And she actually snapped her fingers. "Like *that*, and you will never see her again, I promise you." Then she was asleep again, but I wasn't. I never slept that night.

Nor the next one—not much, anyway. Not only was

there no sight or sound of Jenia, but for the first time we completely lost track of the little stream we'd been keeping on our right. The road veered off directly, not running parallel to the water anymore, but almost doubling on itself, vanishing into a world of flowering trees with bunches of purple leaves like sleepy eyes. I stopped walking and just looked at Dakhoun, once I realized that I couldn't hear the water at all now. She looked back at me without saying anything, without ever breaking stride.

I started to say, "Maybe we ought to think about. . . ." But I stopped, because there wasn't any sense in going on. There wasn't any other road right then; there was just the one under our feet, and all we could do was hope that somewhere, at some point, it would turn back toward the stream and Jenia. Remembering, it seems to me that I didn't have anything like hope or any vision at that point. All I had was plain blind stubbornness. Sometimes that will do.

Oddly, during that long silent walk that took up the rest of the day, I found myself thinking, for once, not even about my mother and father but about Dakhoun's parents, who had loved her against all rules and traditions, and let her just go away on her own. Had they known that she was hunting as doggedly for Death as I was for my sister? I couldn't believe that . . . and yet, when it all came down to it at the last, what did I know about what anybody knew about anything? My mother, still shopping at the market for those little biscuits I used to love . . . my father in the night, always needing to be sure I was home—my father, who had seen me run off to the Dreamies, just as *she* had. . . .

I did stop thinking about that because I finally had to, that second night. And I did sleep then, but I dreamed. Let it go. I slept, and I dreamed, and Dakhoun didn't wake me. Let it go.

VII

WHEN I WOKE UP, IT WAS PAST DIM, BUT not dark, and Dakhoun was gone. But as I scrambled to my feet, fumbling for my boots, I saw the shadows waiting.

There were two of them. One was human looking enough—as Dreamies go, anyway. She might have been some sort of princess, robe and diadem and all, with her cold, elegant face, but for those clawed hands with the extra fingers. She was beautiful, no doubt about it—likely the most beautiful creature I've ever seen. But she frightened me.

The other shadow . . . I can't say what he actually looked like, even now, even when I close my eyes and see him clearly. Not the way that I still see those four men—I always will be seeing them, always, and that's all there is to that. This was different.

He was big. Really *big*, which was odd by itself. Dreamies don't generally run big—I mean, I guess they can if they want to; I don't think they're all the way attached to their shapes, the way we are. But I've almost never seen a Dreamie much bigger than a good-sized human—just that one. He was the size of my mother's old chest of drawers, which even my uncle Ambrose can't reach the top of. . . . He was the size of an elephant, which I've never yet seen. But I know that's how big they are.

Like the other one, the woman, he was handsome in a kind of alarming way. I had the feeling that if he let go, let himself go, he would look much more like an evil *thing* than a charming, friendly man, but he held on most of the way. Just once in a while it would slip for a moment, and then the eyes would glow through. But you had to be looking for it.

I said, "I'm waiting for my sister. I'm not going away." I had to say it twice, because it didn't come out clearly the first time.

The woman—or whatever she was—smiled at me. She had an almost friendly smile. She said, "No. You are not. Not ever."

Not ever finding my Jenia? Not ever getting out of this place—this endless kingdom without a king—never finding my way back to my parents and our goats and stupid sheep? Or did she mean something else, something far worse? Something I hadn't even considered?

"Not until I find her again." I said it very loudly, because I needed boldness very badly just then. "When I do, then we will be on our way, and there will be no chance for anyone to stop us. We are going home together."

The woman never lost her smile, but the big one's face changed. He whispered that thing I remembered the fish-toothed boy saying: "*She belonged to us before she was born. . . .*" But then he added—no louder, but terribly clearly, "And so do you. So do you."

The woman gave him a quick, sharp glance, as though she had warned him not to say that. Then they were both gone, vanished, and then I had to sit down because my legs wouldn't work anymore. They'll usually do what I ask for, but boldness always costs.

I was on my feet when Dakhoun returned, I know that. She appeared out of the early dawn with a double armful of some kind of bright scarlet fruit whose name I can't ever remember. They don't grow where we live, and I don't really *like* them, but I do have a sort of taste for them, if you understand, and Dakhoun always picked them out. I said idiotically, "Where have you been? They were just here!"

"I know." Dakhoun remained as calm and expressionless as she always was. "I saw them."

I started to ask, "Did you hear what he said? What he told me?" Then I stopped. I'm not exactly sure why I bit the words back, except for the aggravation of knowing that, for all the time we'd been journeying together, I could still never find out what was truly going on in that stone woman's head. From the terrible night we met, she had followed me uncomplainingly down every road I wandered in this endless, mocking place in search of my sister, Jenia, and I knew I owed her far more than she had ever asked me to pay back. And even so, even so . . . somewhere, I'd given up on learning who she was. She could follow me forever, or turn around where she stood and walk away out of my sight, never looking back and gone. And I would never understand why, any more than I knew now.

So I just said, "Oh. Well, we should be on our way. Thank you for the fruit—I'll eat it as we go."

I did, too, all of it. As I said, it grew on you, in a way.

Maybe it was a little like the land of the Dreamies itself. No, that's not right—I never for a minute grew easy or comfortable in that uncanny country, not ever. But if I never go back there—and I never, ever will—still it has some kind of hold on me, and I know it, and knowing it frightens the midnight sense out of me to this day. But I know what my father just glimpsed there, although he never actually saw the land of the Dreamies himself. And I thought I knew why Jenia thought she belonged there, and wouldn't come home with me. It turned out I was wrong about that, but there you are.

We didn't see any sign of her that day, or the next, nor much of the Dreamies themselves, either. It was low country we were passing through, so there weren't many trees—as I've told you, Dreamies really like trees—and I could tell that a lot of the ground would be too damp for them. I liked it myself, because there were all sorts of flowers everywhere you looked, purple and yellow bright enough to hurt your eyes, and there were multicolored bushes looking as though they'd just been splashed with paint that morning, right before we got there. Some of those might almost have been young new birds or great butterflies, about to go dancing into the air if you waited a moment. It wasn't at all what we were searching for, but it was pretty. I do have to say that.

We always found some dry spot for our blankets and to settle into without much conversation. I remember saying once, without any warning, "I'm not giving up, you know that."

Dakhoun nodded, not ever turning her head, and replied, "I never thought you were."

And I repeated, louder, "Well, I'm just not, however long." Dakhoun nodded again, and that was all for that night.

And then that forever road dipped down sharply, and then it banked gradually to the right—I just remember groves of things almost like willows, only different—and then it swooped straight up and shook itself, like a horse trying to throw us off its back, and then it leveled off . . . and there she was. Oh, there she was.

She was with a little group of Dreamies—not many, they looked like more at first, the way they clustered around her. But I would have known her in an instant, even at that distance. She was by herself among them, if you understand me, walking alone, turning briefly to one side or another, but not actually talking with anyone. I began to walk faster.

At my shoulder, Dakhoun said only, "Remember."

I stopped where I stood. The stone woman said nothing further; only held my eyes calmly with her pale ones, unreadable as ever, waiting. I said, "I know. I'll remember. But I do have to try."

The last few words came out in a mumble, and I don't know whether Dakhoun heard them or not. I went on without looking back, doing my best to move as slowly as Jenia. She saw me coming to her, and even from that distance I could see her body tensing to run. I honestly didn't know what I'd do if she did, whatever Dakhoun had said. But instead she made herself turn back toward me and simply waited until I reached her.

She didn't put her arms around me this time, but she did smile cautiously, watchfully. For my part, I didn't clutch at her, though all the gods know I wanted to. I don't even remember smiling at her. She finally spoke my name, and nothing more. "*Sooz . . .*"

I said, "Our mother misses you."

She shook her head, still smiling patiently. "She's your mother. Not mine."

"You have it backward," I said. I kept my voice down, but the Dreamies were drifting gradually toward us, the way they'd done before. I said, "You were born of her, you came out of her belly. I came in a basket on her doorstep—me and Malka. Did you ever know that?"

Such a stupid, stupid question; how could she have known, who never looked back? But it went home—I could see that in her eyes, and in the sound of her breath. She started to answer, but her voice was too low and I couldn't make out the words. I came closer, not ever looking at Dakhoun, whom I knew had ranged up behind me.

I said, "Your father saw you run away with the Dreamies when you were four years old. We only call them that because that's what you always called them. Do you remember?" When she said nothing, I asked again, "Do you remember that day? Because your father never will forget it until he dies. He walks the house at night when he can't sleep, looking in my room to make certain I'm there. I always hear him."

"Sooz," Jenia said. For the first time, her voice sounded like someone else's voice, someone trying to speak another language. "Sooz, don't."

But I kept on talking, because I had to. I had to. My own voice was starting to come apart at the edges, though I tried and tried to hold it steady. "I know you remember. Talk to me." She turned her face away. I still didn't grab her, but I came so close that I could smell her, smell her breath, which pierced me like winter chill. I said, "I never learned about you at all, because they couldn't bear to speak of you. *He* only remembers your birthday party, and how happy you looked when the Dreamies were swinging you by your arms, the way *they* used to. Do you remember?" And, yes, now I was screaming at her, no denying it, even with Dakhoun looking at me. *"Do you remember?"*

The Dreamies were pushing in between us, actually separating me from Jenia. I didn't care, I just kept screaming, "Do you remember *who you are?*" She wouldn't turn back toward me.

A very small male Dreamie—he looked a bit like an angry old baby—kicked me in the legs without warning, and I fell to my knees. I never saw Dakhoun move, but I saw him go flying as she raised me quickly to my feet. She made no sound, but her teeth were bared.

I wrenched myself away from Dakhoun's grip, still gasping, still trying to catch my breath. I shouted as loudly as I could over the heads of all those crowding Dreamies, "This is not your home! This is not where you live!"

Suddenly she was facing me, forcing her way between those scattery clumps of creatures who looked like people. They weren't exactly resisting her, but they were making a sort of fire sound, a crackling to themselves. She paid them no attention; they might as well not ever have been there. "I can't go home, Sooz. I couldn't dare."

She didn't say, "I wouldn't dare." I'd have noticed that. "I *couldn't* dare" is different. I didn't exactly notice the difference then, I only knew something wasn't right.

"What are you talking about?" I demanded. "Of course you can go home! *They're* waiting for you—they've always been waiting for you! And you've *always* known!" That's what made me so angry, I realized that as I threw it at her. Not how long she'd been gone, not how long a journey I'd come on after her—none of that mattered at all, not now. But that she'd clearly *known*. . . .

"Sooz." Her voice was thin and ragged, but very clear, the only voice in the world among all the chattering around her. "Sooz, I was four years old."

I didn't understand. "I know you were. My mother told me about your birthday party. Your cousins came."

She didn't cry—none of them ever did, not ever—but her eyes were wet. She said, "Now I am twenty-one years old."

I said, "I'm seventeen."

Several Dreamies—two or three of them big enough to look threatening; another so old and pale and shapeless

that I couldn't be sure whether it was male or female—
came pushing at me, trying to force me away from Jenia.
But I wouldn't go, and Dakhoun made a sound that made
them think about it. All my attention, in that moment,
was fixed on Jenia.

"They have always remembered my birthday, even when
I forgot it. When I turned twenty-one they told me . . ."
She hesitated for the first time. "Sooz, they told me that I
could choose."

"Choose *what*?" I asked. "And who's *they*?"

I wasn't going to like either answer, I already knew
that. Right then I didn't care. That's true. I was so tired,
and I really didn't care.

Jenia took a deep breath before she spoke again, and I
could hear her trying to keep her voice as even as she
could. She said, "I don't have to grow any older than I am.
I can live forever, if I want to."

I didn't understand. I just stared at her.

My sister said, "Everyone here, all the ones you see,
they've all decided who they are, *what* they are, how they
choose to be seen. They can be any age they want, any
sex, any species. You know this, Sooz. You've seen them."

I took a quick glance at Dakhoun, standing a little way
behind me, saying nothing, showing nothing. I think I
wanted her to interfere, to shake her head fiercely and
assure me that I wasn't hearing what I couldn't be hearing. No help there; she was occupied with keeping the

Dreamies off Jenia and me, and looking dangerous. I managed, weakly, "I don't understand."

For the first time Jenia looked some way embarrassed. She said, "Sooz, listen to me. I have to decide whether I want to be immortal." She faced me almost defiantly; she actually stamped her foot, the same way I used to do myself when I was little and really mad about something. I have to say that she looked better than I did at those times—I always get red in the face, and I splutter a lot. My sister just looked even more beautiful.

But I saw no happiness or triumph, not when our eyes met directly. The rest of her, yes—the tumbly-soft hair, the glowing light brown skin; that way of carrying herself, as though she'd never ever have to think about being ugly or alone or afraid . . . she might almost have been designed to suit my parents. Or my relatives, even stupid Uncle Ambrose. I remembered what I'd thought, that very first time, over Malka's grave: *She looks more like family than I do. . . .*

Not the eyes. Those gray eyes had become a stranger's eyes, so terrified that it took me a while to recognize them at all. Jenia whispered, kept whispering. "I don't know. . . . I don't know. . . ."

"What?" I demanded. "You don't know if you want to stay here, in this place you ran away to? Or you want to come home to the place where you're supposed to be? Tell me now, and let's be done!"

I didn't know what she'd answer. All I know is that I was terribly afraid of it, and I had to sound as though I didn't care. That's always been the hardest thing in the world for me. I don't think I've ever once gotten the sound right.

Jenia's voice was clearer, but still shaking. "Sooz . . . Sooz. I wouldn't ever die. They told me I'll live forever. . . . They said I was always meant to be their queen—"

I'm not proud of what happened then. I don't have a single excuse for it. I screamed at her at the top of my voice. "That's what they promised you? That you're the born queen of this place—Dreamieland, the Fae, whatever they call it—that you'll reign here forever? That's it, that's what you want? Well, if that's what you really want, then good luck to you, and I'll just go on home. You never belonged with us anyway! You never ever did!"

I turned on my heel and walked away from my sister, the sister I'd never known even existed—the sister I'd come so far at such a cost to find. She called my name, but I never once looked back. Not that I'd have been able to see her, anyway, blind as my eyes were. Dakhoun held my arm, and guided me.

I think Dakhoun looked back once—I could feel it— but I don't know.

VIII

I CAN'T SAY MUCH ABOUT THE REST OF THAT DAY. Sometimes I walked by myself; other times, Dakhoun was there when I suddenly had to sit down. That happened a couple of times, but Dakhoun never broke the silence—only found a safe place in the shade for me, and waited until I was ready to go on. Three times, it was, not two. That much I remember.

And I couldn't tell you much about where we spent the night, either. I remember warmth, and that same silence. All I did was lie on my back and stare up at the empty sky, and wait for morning. I thought about my sister a little, but mostly I thought about how big the newborn kids must have grown by now. How long had I been gone? It might have been a minute, or a hundred years, or any time at all. I kept seeing the kids, grown now, dropping newborns of their own behind rocks, jumping and capering the way goats do. I missed them more than anyone that night. Dakhoun went out twice, hunting, but she came back empty-handed.

I don't think she slept any better than I did. She had her eyes closed most of the night, but that didn't ever mean anything. I let my eyes fall open when I heard her moving around restlessly, and saw her on her feet, looking back the way we had come. She said very softly, "We have to go back."

She can't have meant me to hear her, but I heard. "We have to do *what*?"

I didn't even know I was up and loud until Dakhoun turned to me, and I saw how startled she was. I said, "Not a chance. Not a chance in the world."

Dakhoun never raised her voice. She almost never did, which was one of the most annoying things about her. But I'd learned to read those strange pale eyes when I bothered to pay attention. "Sooz. Listen to me. If you want to see your home again, we have to retrace our path and start over. There is no other way." I opened my mouth, but she cut me off before I'd even taken a breath. "And, yes, you will have to take my word. I do know what I am telling you. I know, Sooz."

And *I* knew she was right, and there wasn't a chance in the world that I was going to admit it. Knowing hasn't anything to do with the way you behave—at least, not when it comes to me. I can't apologize. I'm tired of apologizing.

"No," I said. "Just *no*. You go back, you go on wherever. I know a few things myself." My voice wasn't a voice I'd ever heard in my life. "What would you know about going home, anyway? You don't have any idea what a home's like! You never *had* a real home, you wouldn't know home if you fell over it! You just drag along, drag along, looking for Death, and he can't even be bothered with you!" I couldn't stop. I swear I couldn't stop. "You don't belong anywhere at all! And I'm sorry for you, I really am."

She didn't even blink. She just stood there, looking at me. And while she was looking at me, and while I was still yammering, I learned a terrible thing.

The worst thing in this world is not to lose all you have. The worst thing in this world is not having your heart broken. Loss passes, pain passes—even heartbreak passes. The very worst thing in this world is to hurt a heart that cares for you. I know that now.

The really worst part is that I knew that then. I just didn't have the words for it. But I knew it in my own heart.

Dakhoun turned and walked away, back toward the way we had come. She never said a word, and she never looked back. Her back was as straight as ever. I watched her to the road, and then I followed. Just because I'm a fool, that doesn't mean I'm an *idiot*. Not the same thing.

I took longer than I should have to catch up with her. When I finally did, I stayed a few strides behind her, the same way she usually walked with me, and I kept a little to the side. She never looked at me, not once. I didn't say a word in all that time.

She knew exactly where we'd lost the road. I'd never have known, except for the Dreamies. We'd hardly seen even a one on our way the night before; now there were more and more of them as we walked on, stalking us, mocking us, or insisting on accompanying us. Sometimes they looked like people I'd seen before—the fish-toothed boy was always there, and that beautiful woman who had a way of smiling at me that I always wished she wouldn't— and other times they might have been perfectly ordinary human beings, except that they were Dreamies, and they never quite looked right. But I was used to them, so most of the time it didn't bother me the way it did before. Most of the time, anyway.

When Dakhoun suddenly stopped short, hesitated, and then carefully turned aside, there were a good dozen or more of them, loudly crowding us away from where she meant to go. I had to push up beside her to hear her when she said, "This is our way."

The Dreamies were all shouting. "No road! Forbidden! No road! Can't go!" In all our time in that country, I'd never heard them sounding shrill, alarmed, even panicky. I thought it might be because there actually *wasn't* any road; it was a sort of bluff that we'd have to scramble up to go on wherever we were trying to get to. Once or twice Dakhoun stumbled, and I had to reach back for her hand; more often, weary as she was, she was the one who held me steady until I could brace my feet, catch my breath, and go on. Either way, we were both exhausted by the time we reached the top of that bluff.

The Dreamies didn't follow us there. A couple of them did make it up to the top, nudging and chattering all the way, but they dropped back down quickly, chasing each other through the brush like squirrels. Dakhoun and I trudged on, me still keeping safely behind her, still half hoping she'd speak to me, and half-afraid she would. It's purely awful to feel that way about someone you're with. I got so I'd almost have settled for those Dreamies again.

The land we were passing through wasn't like any country I'd seen before. It was all dark, not-quite-stagnant water to the horizon, with stumpy roots bulging up like great knees, covered with strange soft bark. I reached out to touch one or two as we went by, and drew my hand back in a hurry. Whatever it was, it didn't feel like bark. It felt as though it wanted my hand.

We didn't ever really stop to rest. There wasn't much point to it, and there definitely wasn't any place we'd have wanted to sit down. Nothing beyond the long, wide water

was really wetland, but neither was anything ever properly dry, if you understand *dry*.

We finally settled under a leafless gray tree, and did
what we could with my damp cloak. Of course I offered
to make room for Dakhoun, and of course she wouldn't
share mine. All she said was that she didn't need it, and
that was that.

And that was that, until toward dawn . . . toward
what must have been dawn, she did at last fall asleep. I lay
awake awhile longer until I was sure, until she was breathing with the least little bit of a whistle, the way she does.
Then I eased my cloak over her, hoping vaguely that some
of my night's warmth might linger for her. And then . . .
then I took a breath myself, and laid my right arm across
her very lightly, ready to snatch it back at any moment,
pretending that I'd just been turning in my own sleep,
and I whispered, "Please. I'm sorry."

She didn't stir, but she didn't move away from me either. So we just lay like that, in the damp dark, and finally
I fell asleep myself.

We must have slept a long time, because we woke up
more or less in the same position where we'd fallen asleep.
We sat up and stared at each other, for the longest time in
the history of the world that any two people ever stared
at one another. For all I know, we'd still be doing it, except that I sneezed, and then I started the shivering, the
silent shaking that you can't ever name or control. And I

know I'd still be doing it right now, only for Dakhoun putting her arms around me.

It doesn't matter what she said, what I said, or how long we actually sat there together, just looking. There's a point where you can't even shiver anymore—you plain run out of bones to hurt, and then convulsing becomes choking, and then it becomes gasping, and then it's wheezing, and so on. I'm grateful today that I didn't throw up, because that's the very next step, and at that point I was already lying with my head in Dakhoun's lap. So it could have been a lot worse, believe me.

Dakhoun said, "You are hungry," and I shook my head. But I *was* hungry, and of course she knew it. So nothing would do but she had to go off by herself and hunt up *something* for me to eat. I didn't recognize it, but I got it down while she watched me. And we set off walking again, silent as ever but side by side.

That swamp, or whatever it really was, went on forever, or anyway most of that day. Toward sundown, the ground started to rise under our feet—no dramatic swoops or drop-offs, just a slow, exhausting climb. Dakhoun didn't say anything much—it wasn't at all necessary, and besides she was very plainly too busy catching her breath. Which was another worry for me as we went on.

She was still strong, much stronger than I ever was. Maybe it came simply from being made of stone; maybe it came from inside her, some way, just being so powerful in who—or what—she was, so silently fierce that she always caught me when I fell. But for all that, she no longer had the endless, tireless reserves of air and ease that I'd come to rely on without thinking about it.

Now I understood that I'd been watching over her—*how long had it really been?*—just the way she'd kept such a careful eye on me since that night she found me, alone and half-mad with fear and rage and pain under the moon. I wanted to tell her, as we panted our way up and down and up again, "It's all right, I'm here, I'll take care of you. I will." But I would never say that to Dakhoun, never. Even I know that, at least.

All the same, she was most often the one gripping my hand to haul me up a stony, skiddy stretch where my feet couldn't brace themselves at all, or coaxing me over a wide ravine my stomach just didn't want to think about. I mostly made sure that she rested often by telling her I was tired. I was never any sort of a hunter, but there were little sunburnt plants and leaves you could eat, if you didn't think much about them. And I did get good at listening for the little trickly streams here or there along our way. I brought water in the canteen; even in my hands a few times, when it was so dark I couldn't see the stream itself.

It was a lot easier to find some dry place to sleep here, so there was that. There were shallow caves, or places where a few boulders had slid together to form something like half a roof and a couple of walls. We stayed almost warm by sleeping as close as we could; and if sometimes I woke up shivering, Dakhoun would turn and hold me awhile until my body quieted. She herself never felt the cold, nor ever once was frightened, so far as I knew.

But *lonely*. . . . How could she not have been lonely, the only surviving one of her kind, all the others killed straightaway at birth? As far as I ever knew, whatever she knew of love came from her own mother and father, the ones who kept her and protected her, until she ran away for their sake, to protect *them*. For anything else . . . for anything else, there was just me, and by now you know what depending on me is like. And so did she.

After a day or two, the high hills began slowly dropping away, though you couldn't ever trust them not to rear up on you and force you to start climbing all over again. Even so, the ground was plainly leveling off, which was good, because my legs had begun to wobble like the legs of a newborn lamb. Dakhoun went along as always, keeping her regular even pace; you would have to be closer than either she or I would have let you come to notice the *thing* in her breathing that might be a catch or just the smallest possible extra breath . . . or might not be, you'd been wrong. Dakhoun gave nothing away, not ever.

The land finally settled into being desert, increasingly, pitilessly dry. At first, there was a little water here and there, and then there was none at all; at first, there were a few small, scattered growing things, even a few very small things like lizards and snakes and mice scampering around and eating each other. And finally there wasn't anything at all, and Dakhoun and I went hungry.

Hungry I know about. I know about famine times, and I remember my mother dividing one last loaf of bread among the four of us, or managing a dinner out of carrots grown soft with being out of the ground too long and a few tired old turnip greens. There had been plenty of nights on the road in search of my sister when I'd cried myself to sleep, weeping for sorrow that my family would never find my body because I'd be lost forever among these empty hills and foggy waterfalls. But somehow in a day or two—three days once, just the one time—I'd stumble on water somewhere, and where there was water there'd be *something* growing near enough. And that was all before Dakhoun came and found me.

But now I was starving. Which was a word I'd never used before, not in the worst of the worst times—but now I said it in my head, because I knew Dakhoun was starving along with me. Not because she was going without food or drink—as she'd said once, so very long ago, "Why should stone eat?"—but because *starving* is what humans do, and I could feel her fear as I never had before. I wanted to tell her not to be afraid, that I was still her friend and I'd always take care of her. Except that wasn't it, I meant to say that we'd take care of each other, because that was what we did. That was always what we did.

The trouble was that I couldn't make anything come out properly. And Dakhoun was carrying me—at some point, anyway. Things blur when you're some way past hungry, so I'm not quite sure when all that was. I do know I made her put me down somewhere, because I could walk like anyone else, I told her that. And then she was carrying me again, or maybe that was the first time. I told you, things blur when you starve.

Then it was dark . . . no, that was maybe the other day when it was starting to get dark, and the sky was so beautiful, the most beautiful sky I'd ever seen, and I didn't mind lying on my back like that. And Dakhoun was stroking my face with her rough hands and whispering, and I don't think she was crying, because stone can't cry, she told me, she did, I remember. And then there was another voice, different, and it was very far away, but I knew that voice, and I tried to sit up and answer, but I couldn't make a sound, and it was my sister.

IX

THERE WAS WATER, AND A HORSE WHINNY-
ing somewhere, and there were voices. The water
kept splashing my lips, so it was hard for me to swallow
it. When I choked, the water was snatched away, and I
heard Dakhoun's angry voice. I'd never heard her sound
angry at all, not in all the time we'd been journeying together. I couldn't make out her words right then, but after a moment the water was touching my mouth again,
gently this time, and Dakhoun was saying, "Slowly, slowly
now, slowly. . . ." I knew her voice still, but it was trembling in a way I couldn't recognize. "If you drink too fast,
it will make you sick. *Slowly* . . ."

It was hard, because my mouth was so dry, so long dry
that it didn't seem to taste the water at all, the way rain

will just bounce straight off desert soil. But Dakhoun was very careful, cupping my face with one hand and tipping the container enough to wet my lips, but not enough to let the water run down my chin. I remember that a couple of drops did, and I lapped at them with my tongue. That was tiring by itself, and I think I might have dozed awhile. I'm not sure.

I woke up, if I really was asleep, when I heard Jenia's own voice, and realized that I'd been hearing it for some time. So I guess I *had* been sleeping, but I couldn't understand anything she was saying; she might have been speaking a completely different language, maybe even singing. It sounds silly, but I think I blinked a lot, listening, as though it would in some way help me listen more clearly.

Jenia was saying, "I brought food. She can have food?" It was a question, but not quite a question. She sounded more like a child than my older sister.

I heard Dakhoun answer shortly, "Give it to me." Her own voice wasn't angry anymore; it had gone back to being expressionless, which I was long used to, and didn't think anything about. But this was flat and cold. That can sound like the same thing, but it isn't. I knew the difference, and I think Jenia did, too.

Something cool and sweet smelling brushed my lips, and Dakhoun said close to my ear, "Eat this very slowly . . . a bite at a time, just so. Just so . . ." I know it was some sort of fruit, but I don't remember what kind; the true taste of it, the texture, all of that is lost, if I ever knew it. I do remember that Dakhoun had her arm under my shoulders. That, yes.

It gets cold at night in desert country, no matter how hot it's been by day. Dakhoun went off to search for whatever might burn, leaving my sister and me to look at each other at last. Which turned out to be much stranger than you'd think because, after all the time I'd spent seeking her through the senseless wonderment of the Dreamies' world—then finding her at last, *then* having to chase her down all over again, only to have her tell me for a second time that she didn't want to come home with me because she was born to be an immortal queen of all the Dreamies . . . well, you would think we'd at least have something to say. You would think.

Staring at Jenia in the twilight wasn't at all like waking up to meet Dakhoun's pale eyes and turn into a shivering baby. My sister was still astonishingly lovely, as beautiful as a life of being cherished by the Dreamies could have made her—to my forever shame, I couldn't help wondering what I'd have grown up to look like if I'd been the child they'd chosen—but somehow it didn't mean anything to me, not the way it should have. I still loved her, and I couldn't ever regret my search, no matter any cost, but I knew a friend worth a dozen of her.

Finally Jenia asked me, almost shyly, "Do you want anything more to eat? You must still be so hungry."

"I don't think so," I said. "I've been picking at bits of this and that all the time. Thank you for bringing so much food with you. It must have been such a burden to carry it all."

"No, I had a horse, I told you." I'd forgotten the soft whinny nearby, somewhere during the evening. I'd almost never seen them among the Dreamies. Jenia said, "Horses belong only to the king. He won't be happy that I took his."

"The king," I said, stupidly enough. "So there is actually a king among the Dreamies. I didn't know."

"No. You couldn't have known. He lives deep in the woods, and he's older than anyone, anyone. I've only seen him once in all the time I've . . . been here." The light was almost gone now, and I could feel the darkness on my skin, the way it always gets in that country. Every night there'd be something with a soft little hiccup of a croon. I can't even say if it was a bird, because there really wasn't anything much in that desert for it to perch on. I never saw it, whatever it was. But we heard it every night while we were there.

I said, "Jenia, do you know how long you've been here? Can you tell me what you actually remember?"

She took a long time to answer. I was slowly coming to learn that she seemed to have two voices, and I couldn't yet tell which one was likely to respond at any moment. One was the voice of the beautiful stranger whom I had never known until the moment I splashed across a stream to meet her at last in this bewildering world where she lived. And she had held me and praised me, and told me that now I must turn around and go back home and tell our parents that I couldn't find her.

The other voice . . . that other was the voice of that little girl who had run off to that world when she was four years old. Now she had chosen to run away again with Dakhoun and me, while she was supposed to become queen of that world and live forever. And that voice was as frightened as my own. I knew that voice.

"I don't know. I'm not sure, not always." She wasn't quite looking at me, but more at a slant, an angle, exactly the way I get when my mother's not likely to be happy with whatever I'm about to tell her. She whispered, "I was four. I wore my special green dress—my froggy green, I always called it. There was a birthday party, I remember, I do. . . ." My breath stopped, just completely. "And it just goes on and on, on and on, and I'm so happy that everything's just the way it's supposed to be, forever . . . and when I think about it, which I never, never do, . . ." Now she did look straight at me, but her eyes were not any eyes I knew. "And just for that moment I suddenly have no idea where I am, who I am, and I'm so scared, and I don't know *anybody*, and it's so cold and it's all turning dreadful, and I'm *scared*, and no one will ever come. . . ."

I could have done something. I could have reached for

her and pulled her head hard to my shoulder, or tried to hold her the way Dakhoun used to hold me whenever I woke up in the night. But Jenia was so far from me, so rigid with fear that she'd never have noticed. And by then she was back being that other one, that beautiful one, and I didn't know what to do.

"Sooz," she said slowly. It seemed to take her a long time just to say my name. "Sooz, I cannot go back to your home with you. I can show you the way there; I can set you on the road, which you will never find by yourself. That I can do—they will let me do that, if I promise to return. Do you understand me?"

"No," I said. I was very loud about it. "No, I don't understand, and I never will! I don't care how long they've kept you, you know you don't belong in that place. There's something you aren't telling me! What aren't you telling me?"

I heard the small sound of Dakhoun's return, but I don't think my sister did. You have to be listening for Dakhoun.

"This land—this world—this *place* is my home," Jenia said. "However you see it, whatever you think of my being here, whatever I . . . whatever I almost remember . . ." She paused for just a moment, but when she spoke again her voice became increasingly firm and determined. "None of that matters—none of it, Sooz. I love you—I loved you before I met you, before you came to find me—but this is where I do belong. Whatever I might have chosen, this is where I belong. This is what I know."

Dakhoun didn't say a word. Jenia took my hands, her own hands now as cool as her voice. "I promised I would set you on your safe road home. It is not my road—it is no longer my real road home—but I will take you there. You have my word, little sister."

Why did those last two words fall so painfully on my skin? She didn't mean them to hurt me—I *know* that, better than anyone else could—but I still hear them, even now. I said only, "Where I go, my friend goes."

"I never said otherwise." Which was perfectly true; she never suggested anything different, but she never once looked directly at Dakhoun, either. She said, "If you should care even to start out tonight . . ."

Dakhoun spoke then, just as evenly as she. "She is not well. We will start the day after tomorrow."

I started to protest, "No, I'm ready right now," but even I knew better than that. If I tried to walk as far as where Jenia's horse was picketed, I'd fall down halfway there. When I finally know something, I do know something.

Dakhoun had actually found something growing in that naked desert. It wasn't green, and it looked as though it had sprung out of the ground burned brittle. But you could eat it, practically, and Dakhoun had gone a long way to bring it to me, and I got all of it down and thanked her, and went to sleep.

I slept most of that next day, too. I know Jenia woke me once to coax me to eat some of the food she had brought with her, but I was practically asleep while she fed me. I think she sat watching me for a long time after I fell asleep. Sometimes you can feel it; I don't know why that is.

That evening I woke up feeling much better, and as seriously hungry as I should be. Yes, I'd dreamed, as I still do today, of those four men who had taught me the road, and who will always haunt my nights. But by now I knew them almost by name—and certainly by that sad little song that will be the last thing I ever remember—and they have become, if hardly friends, simply my old familiars. They come in many different forms, but I always recognize them, so I can deal with them. At the last, they are simply part of the night I met Dakhoun.

Having slept too long that day, of course I had a lot of trouble with the night. Jenia, for her part, had gone to bed quite early, anxious to save her strength for the long journey ahead. She made a point of wishing us both joyous rest and happy waking. So I tossed, and sat up more than once with my arms hugging my knees. Dakhoun's eyes were closed, but I knew she wasn't asleep.

"The horizon's changing," I said aloud. "I mean, we never used to have a horizon at all, night or day. There was never anything to see anywhere, and now there is." I craned my neck, trying to see farther around me. "I can't make out what, but there's definitely something."

"It is her doing." Dakhoun had not opened her eyes. "She is leading us home, as she said she would do. So the land is already different. You will see when the light comes."

"And then what?" I had not known that was going to come out of me; it just leaped out, like blood. "Do you think she might change her mind again?"

You can't really shrug when you're lying down, but Dakhoun managed it all the same, the way she does. "Who can say? I think she has changed her mind many more times than she knows. Go to sleep, Sooz."

"Can't." I mumbled. "Not sleepy." I lay down again, turning on my side. "You know, by the way, if she actually does lead us all the way home, you will have to meet our mother and father. This is not an argument—I'm just telling you."

Dakhoun took just a bit more time than she should have to answer me. "I will stay to meet them. Perhaps, if we arrive there late, I might ask to stay the night." Now she chuckled the least bit, more like a tiny breeze on my face. "That is, if they will allow me."

"You can have my old bed," I told her. It was suddenly nice to think about. "And in the morning, I'll make your breakfast. Before you . . . go anywhere, or whatever. I mean, whatever you, whatever, I mean. You know . . ."

"Yes." Dakhoun did not turn herself, but she reached out to touch my arm. "You must sleep now. It will be a long journey."

I did finally fall sleep, and in the morning, I woke to a different country.

Not completely different—I knew where we still were, and there was the same pale, pitiless desert soil under my feet. But there were green hills visible in the distance now, and I could feel water somewhere near, like a dark humming. And there were birds flying over, which somehow changed everything, just by itself. Birds are rare in the land of the Dreamies—we went days without ever seeing more than two or three in the whole sky. The only common ones I ever saw were something like wild geese, only with hawks' bills and claws, and with either deep red feathers or sunset-green ones. They were beautiful and somehow chilling at the same time, like so much else in this world.

We set off that first day, with me riding Jenia's gray mare, and Dakhoun and my sister walking alongside. I protested that I'd been feeling a good deal better, which was true, but there was no arguing with those two, not that day. We passed gradually into softer country: no higher ground, really, but seeming higher because the sky felt deeper and closer to me. There were animals, too, not only birds—rabbits, and things like rabbits; and I saw creatures that could have been goats like ours, and definitely weren't.

And trees that were nearly like trees the way I remembered trees: tall and slender as saplings, but somehow, they didn't look like saplings. They had dark silver trunks and bright leaves the color I imagined the ocean to be, and where the sun shone right down on them, they glittered like blue jewels. But the trunks, lovely as they were, had a strangely temporary air about them, as though traveling troupes had propped them up for a village performance. As though they could be taken down at midnight, fast, for the next town. I'd never have thought that about trees once.

The day grew a little cooler as we moved on, though the air was still pleasant even after sunset. We camped in a grove of those silver trees, and Jenia unpacked our blankets. By the time Dakhoun returned from hunting up our dinner—a couple of rabbit-things and fruits almost like very ripe persimmons, only with a nasty skin you had to bite into really hard to get at the sweet meat, but worth the work—my sister had a fire going, and I'd scooped out a muddy underground stream with my hands. We had a proper dinner that night, we three.

I'd kept up easily enough during the day, which I was proud of and certainly let the others know it, but even so I curled up in my blanket early that evening. Part of that was simply being tired, but I also thought it would be good to let Dakhoun and Jenia talk quietly between themselves for a while. I'd finally accepted the truth: my strange stone friend would always be the mystery I trusted more than myself. My mother and father would just have to accept what she was—at least for the night or two that she'd be with us. I really didn't want to think about that right then.

Jenia was a completely different matter, and more and more I had to think about her. I *knew* Dakhoun, without ever understanding her—as I've said, that's just different. But I didn't know my sister at all. I'd loved her ever since I first saw her on my seventeenth birthday, before I'd ever heard her name or learned anything about her. But what did that mean to Jenia? Or to me, either, for that matter? And why was I having to learn what love meant—me, young and alone and stupid, stupid, *stupid*, in this terrible country that never ever grew any easier to understand, and never would?

When I woke, sometime into the night, I could see Dakhoun sleeping near me. Which was something she'd taken to doing since that desert time when I was so hungry, and even she couldn't find any food or water for me. Jenia was awake, though, pacing slowly back and forth in the moonlight. Now and then she'd look toward the horizon, but not in any particular direction, and not as though she expected to see anything coming to her. She was merely on her feet, and she was talking to herself. I couldn't hear a word, but I saw her face.

I closed my eyes quickly, but I'm sure she knew I was awake. I turned over quickly, too, which gave me away as much as anything. But she didn't speak or approach me;

she just stopped talking and moved to the shadows beyond what was left of the fire. I was planning to keep awake, but the next thing I knew it was bright day.

The days that followed were more or less the same. The landscape kept changing, as it had always done since I first crossed that wandering border, wherever it might be now. I insisted on the others riding at least as much as I did, but mostly I kept prodding Dakhoun, in one way or another, to take my place in the saddle. Which meant that she kept walking that much more, because that was who she was. But I went on insisting that she should be the one riding, because that turned out to be who I am.

I was increasingly worried about Dakhoun. No, *worried* means something else, something difficult, something you can manage somehow. I was truly frightened for her, helpless in a way I had never been in my life. Whether she walked or rode, her weariness came from another place than that stone body that could not be wounded or ever shed blood, or go hungry . . . a place I knew I could never reach. If she hardly ever stumbled on the road, even now, if she never once sagged forward in the saddle, still I knew what I knew. And I would have given my soul, without any question, not to know it. Gods, if you can hear me, I still would.

Jenia knew, too, in her different way. If Dakhoun spoke less and less on the road, my sister talked to me more as we journeyed, almost as though by way of company. Walking beside me, she would point out a sparkling lake or a blue hillside on our way, saying, "Do you remember—you surely must have come this way?" Again, when a long dark creature I have no words for loped across our way, giving us a quick look that set her horse nearly bolting, she clapped her hands and cried in delight, "Oh, Sooz, how wonderful! How lucky you are to see one! In all my time——" And here she stopped herself for a long moment, before she added lamely, "Well, I've only seen one, or perhaps two. They are extremely rare." She told me the Dreamies' name for it, but I never seem to get it right.

The days were growing warmer, and the sun lasted longer, and Jenia kept us traveling while there was light. I'd long since stopped concerning myself about whether or not she was leading us exactly where we needed to be taken. What I couldn't tell, even now, was whether she was deciding to journey all the way home with me, or to turn back at the last to the world that knew her—the kingdom of wonder waiting for their undying spring queen. I knew then, and I know now, that the Dreamies always keep their promises, in their own way.

Dakhoun slept more often now, no matter how easily she had been walking or riding with the rest of us during the day, she who had needed little sleep, or none at all. I'd been off finding a secure place to tether Jenia's mare—property of the king or no, she was born to wander, that one—and I was crouching to rearrange Dakhoun's blanket without disturbing her, when I saw the little dark man.

He seemed to come straight from the night itself, from shadow made flesh. One minute, he wasn't there; the next, sitting close by her, almost on her shoulder, staring hard into her sleeping face. He barely noticed when I tried to brush him away, like a bug. His face was like a dry leaf, and his voice sounded like the first whisper right before the wind comes. "Go away, child. Go to sleep."

"Go away yourself," I said. "You can't have her. This is my friend."

Was I frightened? I don't think so. I don't think I had time. I actually pushed at him, getting myself between him and Dakhoun. He felt like whispering, like a memory of breath. I said again, "She can't die. You don't have any claim on her. Stone can't die!"

He did turn and look straight at me then, in the same way he'd been staring at her, right into my eyes. And, yes, *then* I was frightened, because that dead-leaf face was so dreadfully pitying. He whispered, "Child . . . stone cannot love, either, and yet sometimes it does. Sometimes, even stones . . ."

Whatever I heard, whatever I saw in his face, I wasn't hearing or seeing any of it. I just kept blindly pushing him away. "You go away! You go away from my friend right now!"

And he did. He stood up from Dakhoun—who had

not stirred in her sleep, not once—and he made the strangest little bow, stiff and solemn, and he smiled at me. Then he was gone, leaving me sitting beside Dakhoun, making a sound I didn't know I was making, until I felt my sister's arms around me.

I stopped. I did. Yet I kept hearing it, that sound, and it seemed to take forever—it *did* take forever—until I realized that it was my sister Jenia, making it, making that sound while she held me. We held each other, then.

X

THE TROUBLE WASN'T THAT JENIA'S MARE HAD
pulled her tether loose—I could easily spy where
she'd wandered off to, just by the hoofprints, the munched
leaves, and her droppings—but that she'd somehow gotten
the tether itself tangled in the bunchy, bristly undergrowth. By the time I got her loose and led her back to our
camp, it was nearly dawn and Dakhoun was starting out to
look for me. And the little dark man from the night before
was sitting on her shoulder.

I didn't know what to do. She plainly didn't notice him
at all, didn't feel his weight, didn't even hear him when he
whispered in her ear, no more than she heard me ordering
him to let her be. When she saw me coming back with the

mare, just for a moment, her face turned to sunrise. That was truly when I knew.

And the little dark man knew I knew. For that same moment he seemed to swell up proudly, grandly, bigger than both of us, bigger than the mare that my sister had stolen from the king. Then he was gone, completely, like a sigh, and I heard myself saying, "She got caught in a bramble bush, that's all. You didn't need to come out for me."

Dakhoun's face was as closed and calm as it had ever been. "I thought you might need help. She is not always an easy horse."

"If I can handle her she's an easy horse, believe me." I said, "You slept well?" Dakhoun nodded. No suggestion— none—that she had just been ridden mercilessly herself by a creature who might feel pity for her, but no kindness at all.

"We must be on our way early," she said. "I am certain you can smell your home by now."

Actually, I couldn't. This land of the Dreamies was turning increasingly lovely—even friendly, if you like— but it wasn't any more my own than it ever had been. Maybe when we crossed the border, maybe then there'd be a recognizable wind, an unmistakable taste to the air, a tree or a house or a voice I knew. I just smiled and shook my head a little. "No," I said. "No, not quite yet."

I insisted that it was her turn to ride, and Jenia agreed, even though Dakhoun protested, as she always did. So the two of us walked to the side of the gray mare, while new trees kept springing into being to left and right of us, colored now like wedding dresses and dawn bouquets. After a time Jenia began singing softly, almost to herself.

Up a tree and down a hill,
apple butter, apple spill,
swing three times around the oak,
morning music, midnight joke . . .

I knew that song. It was one my father had sung to me. My father remembers far too many of those songs on the nights when he can't sleep, which is how I know them, hearing him through the walls, just singing. I must have done something with my eyes or my face, because presently she stopped singing. She said, "What?"

"Nothing changes," I said. "It all gets prettier and prettier, but it's still the same. Dakhoun thinks it's you changing everything, but it's not you, is it? Tell me."

My sister was silent. She seemed to shrug away from me with her whole body, like the king's stolen mare when she just didn't feel like being saddled that morning. I said, "It's them, always. Whatever you want, whatever you maybe want, it's them—*it*—the king, I don't know. You can't change anything by yourself. You don't have the power." I stopped walking, stood still in that beautiful morning. "Tell me, Jenia."

The mare kept on ambling ahead. Dakhoun never looked around, and neither did my sister. I had a vision of them keeping on ahead, never turning, saying nothing, until I was out of sight forever. In that moment, of all things, that song of my father's kept going on in my head, like a charm. *"Swing three times around the oak . . ."* Even I know that oaks are magic.

Jenia finally spoke to me, over her shoulder. "I am leading you the right way. You have to believe me, Sooz."

"I do," I said. "But there's more to it than the right way, isn't there?" I began to walk faster, not so much to catch up with her and that horse as to make sure she heard me. My voice didn't sound like me, but like the voice of an old woman I'd never met. "What am I missing, Jenia?"

Ahead of her, Dakhoun suddenly stopped the mare, saying, "It is too beautiful a day to be riding." She slipped out of the saddle as gracefully as a child, and as she did so the little dark man was walking beside her. Sometimes you could see him clearly, sometimes not exactly, just almost. But he was there with her.

Dakhoun paid him no attention. She was picking wildflowers along the road—one more thing I'd never seen her do. She didn't bother with any special type or pattern: some were this color, some that; some of them I recognized, others I'd never known in this world or the one I hoped I remembered. Dakhoun picked them all in great double handfuls, pressing them to her face and smiling with her eyes closed, as the little dark man smiled while he watched her.

Jenia said, "Your way home is on the other side of the way you came. It is different for everyone, but I can take you as far as your own crossing . . . the place where you made up your mind, do you see, Sooz? Do you see?"

I shook my head. "No, but don't worry, I'll just have to know when I get there." Dakhoun was arranging her flowers, just being happy with them—even almost silly, which I'd never seen Dakhoun be before. I asked my sister, "When we do find that place—my crossing—will you be coming with me? I mean, with us?"

The mare was taking the moment to crop whatever grass she could reach. Jenia turned her back to adjust the saddle blanket and swiftly mount. I wasn't sure whether she had heard my question, so I asked it a second time. When she didn't respond, I took it for an answer, and left it alone. We three walked on.

Sometimes there were four of us. The little dark man came and went as he chose, walking next to Dakhoun, or on occasion riding on her shoulders like a weary child. He never looked at me at all now, but from time to time he whispered in her ear. Once in a great while I could see her make a slight face of annoyance, or shake her head irritably; otherwise she never once responded to him, but only clung to her wildflowers. They seemed to blossom all over again in her arms, almost reaching for her themselves, if that makes any sense. It didn't to me, then.

When I spoke to her myself, she answered in short words, no more than she had to. A long time ago—how long? who was I in those days?—I'd never have thought to ask after her health, or whether she needed to ride again. Now I bit back questions like those, only offering her water or one of our few remaining sea-sweets, which she loved as much as she loved any food. And at night . . . at night I stayed long awake beside her.

One thing that did change, day by day, was that we began to see more of the Dreamies. Since the bad time in the desert when I went so hungry for so long, we hadn't seen one Dreamie, not since Jenia came to find us. Now there were more of them every day, usually morning or evening, practically falling out of the trees to keep us company. Sometimes they came looking almost like relatives, people you'd known all your life, except for getting this or that part terribly wrong. At other times they really might have been true dreams, our wild companions, beautiful or terrifying or both together . . . all of it together, all together. And the gods can forgive me or not, as they will, but I finally understood why my sister didn't want ever to come home. And I couldn't blame her.

But the little dark man wasn't any Dreamie. He was there whether I saw him or not, and he grew clearer to my eyes every day, whether walking with Dakhoun like her own special companion or riding her like her master. Either way, she never seemed to see him, even when he spoke to her so clearly that I could make out a word or two myself. Once I heard him say, "*my reasons,*" and another time, "*should you concern . . .*" And I would swear to this day that there was something about "*the dog was an accident. . . .*" The dog? What could he ever have had to do with my Malka? But she paid him no more heed than before. All her attention was on those unfading wildflowers she'd picked.

At night, whether or not the little dark man was anywhere near, she tucked them carefully against her under her blanket. I know that because I so often rearranged the blanket when she turned restlessly or pushed it away. In those moments my hand sometimes brushed Jenia's hands, and even if we didn't speak, we would smile at each other. Dakhoun never woke.

One warm night, which smelled sweetly of rain coming, my sister and I went for a walk together. It wasn't planned; neither of us wanted to be anywhere distant from Dakhoun, but we'd never once spoken of that, nor about anything else unsafe. We talked mostly about daily changes in the landscape—that day it had been winding stretches of moorland, with sudden sunlit pools appearing out of nowhere—and we spoke of odd plants and animals glimpsed along the way, some of which even Jenia had never seen before. "They do that all the time," she said lightly. "You've seen it yourself by now. Some things stay more or less the same, but most things. . . ." She twitched her right shoulder, the same way I do, though she'd never noticed it. "They change."

Neither of us said anything for a bit. I kept glancing back toward Dakhoun, watching for the little dark man. Jenia finally cleared her throat. "I cannot be quite sure, but I do think that tomorrow should bring us at last to the place where you changed your mind. The place where you crossed from your world into . . ." She did not finish.

"Yes," I said. We went on walking.

"You will find your way, I promise," my sister said. "Once you cross the boundary, everything will become directly familiar. You will see." She laughed brightly in the warm night. "Oh, I promise you, dear Sooz, from that moment you will recognize everything that leads you home. Even the goat path, even that windmill Father was always having to repair. . . ." She corrected herself quickly. "*Our* father, I'm sorry."

"Don't be sorry," I said. "He built a new one later—a neighbor friend helped. You couldn't have known."

We didn't say anything after that, until we were almost back at our campground, where I could see Dakhoun turning in her sleep and the little dark man flickering on and off, like a poorly made candle, as he watched her—or watched over her? No, I didn't think that then;

he vanished so quickly as I started toward her that for an instant I expected her to vanish herself.

Jenia said very quietly, "The old windmill . . . those infections the sheep used to get in the corners of their eyes . . . I remember more than I wish I remembered, Sooz." She said my name again, this time almost as a soft question. I turned back toward her for a moment, but she didn't say anything further.

In the morning the landscape had shifted, first to a great field of black sand seeming to flow in every direction, and then gradually away into what must have been a sort of jungle. There were lots of vines wrapping themselves thickly around trees and lacing up into great green ceilings soaring out of sight; there were mounds like huge anthills in every direction, and I could halfway make out muffled loops of a river the color of rain. The Dreamies had mostly fallen back by now, but we could hear their voices in the trees, chattering and laughing, still sounding close by. I wondered whether I would still hear them when I had truly found my way home.

It was really Dakhoun's turn to ride, but it was always harder to get her to agree to that, so I walked behind with her while Jenia rode on ahead. When the little dark man blinked into sight, I blocked his way before he could flicker to her shoulders. "Look at her!" I demanded of him. "Look at her, walking like the rest of us, mile after mile, never ill, never complaining, stronger than anyone!

Oh, you've made a mistake—she doesn't belong to you, she'll never be one of yours, not ever! I'll never let you have her!" I was trying hard to keep my voice low, but I might have been howling those last few words. Just those few, really.

The little dark man looked directly at me for a second time, with that same awful cold pity in his eyes. He said nothing—he never did speak to me again—but only touched my mouth with his hand for just the least instant, and he was gone again.

But I knew he was near, every moment, whether I could see him or not. I spoke to him, very quietly this time, explaining through lips gone suddenly numb. "No, you see, she has to come home to meet my family!" My lips had no feeling for the rest of that day.

It was a long day, that one. The sun never really went down, but just hung there in the sky, while the sky itself actually seemed to be floating away with every hour, growing steadily higher and paler until it didn't feel at all like a real sky, but more of a distant drifting bubble, not connected to anything below. I'd never seen a day like this, even in the country of the Dreamies. The whole day felt swollen around me, as though something bad were going to happen any minute. I wished a storm would break loose, or even maybe a real earthquake, which I've never yet seen. Just to happen, just to have it done.

Dakhoun was finally riding, and I fell into step beside

my sister. The little dark man with his dry-leaf face was nowhere to be seen, and that always made me more nervous than if he were riding on Dakhoun's shoulders. She wasn't eating or drinking at all now—though she still clung to her wildflowers, as though their scent was all the nourishment she needed—and it was harder to rouse her from sleep each morning. Once she was awake, though, she was readier to travel farther then either Jenia or I were, never as eager to rest or to doze even briefly. She never spoke a word to me.

Jenia said quietly, just above a whisper, "Here . . . almost right here. Almost here . . ."

I couldn't see any difference, except that it was finally beginning to grow darker. I said, "Will I know?"

"I told you, it is not the same place for everyone. I never really knew where I crossed the boundary—the Dreamies brought me away, as Father said." She was speaking in that other voice now, the voice that always made her face change. "And *you* . . . you never look where you are going—you just keep going. You see, I have come to know you a little. . . ."

She didn't really smile at me; it was more that her mouth shrugged. "So I imagined just how you would have come running to search for me, imagined where you started from, and how you might have *thought* about someone you never knew. . . ." And then she *did* smile, she did, and for a moment she was my sister, Jenia, all over again. "So. I made certain guesses—and, yes, I made certain inquiries—and now we have followed your path back the way you came, you and I, and your friend."

"Dakhoun," I said. "You know her name."

"Yes, of course," Jenia said. "We three. So here we almost are." She took a short, slow, jagged breath and looked straight and hard at me. "But there are things you have to know before we go any farther. Now. Before you go on."

I only half heard her. The sky was darkening, except where we were. All around us, over us, brightness was rising, as though directly out of the three of us. Meanwhile, the little dark man was constantly whispering to Dakhoun, coaxing and luring her without any pause, never giving her a moment of herself. I had actually taken a step toward him, wanting to slap him, fingers aching to move him away from her—I didn't care *what* he was, not anymore—when Jenia finally caught my attention. I turned back to her, and I just said, "What?"

If I forget my whole life, if I forget every single thing that has ever happened to me, everyone I've ever known, I will always remember Jenia's face then. I will die remembering the way her face began to come apart, just like her voice, like my heart, as I heard her say, "Sooz, you are not my sister."

Of course I knew that. I'd known it since Malka died in my bed and I didn't, even though we'd surely been born together in some basket or other. I think I knew it even before I saw Jenia's dear foreign face. And still I was not going to hear her. *Not.* Not ever, no more than Dakhoun was ever going to hear Death whispering in her ear . . . no more than I was about to pay any heed to that rising light, or to what was happening in me, inside me. Jenia said somewhere, "Oh, Sooz, I wish with all my heart . . ." but I wasn't going to hear that, either, never, not ever.

And then the night broke open, like me, and the king came.

XI

H E CAME AS LIGHTNING. HE CAME AS LIGHT-ning with eyes.

No, that's not what I saw, but not all of it, that couldn't ever be all of it. There *was* lightning, yes, a huge yellow-white flare, only not on the horizon, but so close that I knew thunder had to follow within a bare few seconds. But there wasn't any thunder, just another great flash that left the trees without any color at all, so that everything went black-and-white in that moment, even the leaves on the branches, even the faces of the Dreamies crowding every branch. The only color in the world ever, any-where, was the lightning of the king's eyes.

And I've got the color wrong, too, I'm sorry. Once my own eyes got halfway comfortable, his personal twilight seemed to turn everything ice colored. There's no other way to put the color of those eyes, except that I don't think there's such a color anywhere. You couldn't ever call it *white*, and it's certainly nothing like water or snow, nor anything like silver or steel or any other metal I ever saw. The closest I can come to it is *ice*, and that's not right, either. It's cold as death, and it's deep-down old, like him.

When he spoke, I didn't understand him. It wasn't just that I didn't know the words; it's that he wasn't paying any attention to anyone else but Jenia. And if you don't have the King of the Dreamies' attention . . . then somehow you've stopped existing. No, I don't mean it like that—it's more as though you've lost a whole entire dimension, that's the way I felt right then. No one in the world really existed, except Jenia. Jenia, who used to be my sister . . .

And what he was saying to her was quite clear, words or no words. *"You have no business with such creatures as these. Let them go on their way, and come back where you belong. Come to your family."*

Jenia didn't answer him. I didn't blame her. I saw her face.

The king spoke to her again. I can't say that there was pain in the sound of his voice; all I know is that it was different, some way. He was saying, *"Your family is calling. Come home."* And he spoke her name.

They had their own special name for her, the way

families do. I'll never know what it was, but I heard him speak it to her. You couldn't have missed it.

Jenia still didn't speak, but she was trembling all through her body. I felt it, because I was standing close to her, hoping she could feel me there. She shook her head slightly . . . very slightly, really, but the king knew. He said it one more time. *"You will come home."*

Written down, it looks like a command, but it didn't sound like one. He began to say something else, but just then the Queen of the Dreamies stepped out of his shadow.

It's easier to describe her eyes than his. They were pale, like Dakhoun's eyes, but much lighter, and they had an odd, almost distant quality about them, not as though she wasn't quite there inside them——Nalak, our old ram, has eyes like that——but more as though she'd gotten lost in a very interesting forest, and was thinking seriously about it. Maybe I'd like to have eyes like the Queen of the Dreamies' eyes. I don't know.

At least I had an easier time understanding what she said to Jenia. Maybe it's simply that she was speaking to a daughter, and he was *ordering* a subject. Maybe it's because he loomed over Jenia like a thunderhead, while she didn't appear the least bit bigger or taller than Jenia herself. There wasn't any lightning about her, I know that.

All she said was, *"I miss you."* That's what I remember most about the Queen of the Dreamies.

Jenia said quietly, "I miss you, too." But she didn't call her *Mother* or *Your Majesty*, and she didn't take a single step toward her.

The queen said, "But you are going away with *them*." It was a very little pause just before that last word, but I heard it. I heard it like a bell, or a tiny hammer.

Jenia took a breath before she answered, but there was no hesitation about her voice. "I came away with you a long time ago. It was a beautiful visit, and I'll never be able to say I regret it, but I have to go home now. I will always be grateful for your kindness." And she bowed her head to the queen, just like a gracious lady. A lady of rank.

"Kindness . . ." It wasn't a question yet, but it was definitely more than a little hammer. The queen said, "You do not think that perhaps you found your real home with us." And still not a proper question—she'd known the answer for a long time. Maybe even longer than Jenia knew.

The king spoke then. I didn't understand him any more than I ever did, but I heard the bitterness in his voice as clearly as I'd heard that fish-toothed boy saying, "*She belonged to us before you were ever born. . . .*" But the queen brushed him aside. I never imagined you could do that to the King of the Dreamies.

"We waited for you." She was keeping her voice as firmly under control as she possibly could, but it was struggling in her throat like a wild creature. It was breaking free when she burst out, "We waited longer than your *parents* did!" The way she cried that word made me cover my face. "Longer than *they* ever did! We waited so long for you, so long!"

I felt Jenia shaking beside me, but her voice remained as steady as ever. "I have lived with you almost all my life, and I hardly know those others at all anymore—that is perfectly true. But Sooz . . . Sooz and her friend came to find me without ever having known me, because she knew where I belonged." When I managed to look up, she had taken an urgent pace forward to face the queen close to. "I don't know how she knew this, and I doubt very much that she knows herself. But she knows. That is why I am going home with her." There were tears on her face, but she never bothered with them. "I am very frightened, and I cannot imagine what to expect from these strangers. But it does not matter. I am sorry."

The Queen of the Dreamies did not weep. But she was about to say something more all the same, when the king cut her off. This time there was no arguing with him. You could tell.

"*Come away,*" he said to his wife—and it was his wife he was speaking to, and no queen. "Leave her to the ones she has chosen, to her dog and the walking statue she thinks is her friend . . . to her truest family." The contempt in those words would break your heart, if it weren't already broken by the queen's face. I still wish I hadn't seen that face, those eyes.

"I am no dog." I had to speak up, if I was ever going to make them hear me, because it mattered to me as much as anything ever had. "I am Sooz, that is who I am. This is Dakhoun, my one friend in all this world—and this is my sister, Jenia." I waited for them—and for Jenia—to contradict me, but no one did. "We are going now, back where we came from, by your leave or without it."

I put one arm around Jenia's shoulders, and my other arm around Dakhoun—who looked at me out of those pale eyes as though she had never seen me before—and I started away with those two.

The Dreamies in the trees had been so still while we faced the king and the queen that it was easy to forget they were there, and good riddance, as far as I was concerned. But now they set up a low, whining moan: not the usual teasing chatter—part song, part message, and part plain derision—that I'd grown accustomed to hearing as the daily noise of my life in this strange country. This was a soft, menacing sigh that kept growing gradually stronger. I wouldn't have taken it for a sound that the Dreamies might ever make.

Behind me, the king called out, "Dog? Dog!"

I had to turn then, yes, but only my head, not my whole body, and I never stopped walking. The king said, "You may as well return with us, dog. The life waiting for you and your stone friend will be far less disappointing than any life you might pretend to find where you are bound. You already know this, dog."

I kept walking. I couldn't feel my feet, but I kept on, and so did Jenia. Strangely or not, it was Dakhoun who turned under my arm, turned so angrily that I had to hold on to her with everything I had to keep her from going back to answer the king. It wasn't the first time I had forgotten how strong she truly was. The Dreamies were keening louder each minute, and I missed most of whatever Dakhoun said to me then. I only heard fragments: "He doesn't understand. . . . He doesn't know who you are. . . ."

There was something else—something the queen called after us, but it was lost in the sad racket of the Dreamies. I just kept shoving ahead, never looking back, still trying my best to keep Dakhoun from looking back. She almost wrenched away from me once, but I held on.

Then suddenly it was gone, all the voices all gone, and I stumbled forward when Dakhoun stopped struggling, and I'd have fallen if Jenia hadn't caught me. The moon was rising so fatly that somehow it felt like the only noise there was.

All three of us knew that we had crossed the border, the barrier between one world and that other world— none of us had to say it. We stood still under that swollen, menacing moon for a while, until Dakhoun said slowly, "This is . . . not your home, Sooz."

It wasn't a question. Like the queen, she already knew the answer. I shook my head, and Dakhoun nodded. "Come. I will bring you home."

With that she set off, walking briskly away from the moon. Jenia followed quickly, hurrying to keep up with that stubborn, tireless stride both of us knew so well. But I stood still for a moment, looking vaguely back toward that other place where I had found whom I thought was my sister . . . where I'd lost the girl I thought was me . . . and found the impossible creature I'd come to love. I must have stood there longer than I'd thought, because the sun was well risen by the time I'd caught up with those two.

Things blur when you're as tired and sideways as I know I was, so I can't honestly tell you whether we walked two days or even three. I know that what was blooming all around us was perfectly pleasant, but none of it was quite as familiar as it should have been. I heard the sound of falling water, as reassuring as the smell of growing things in every direction, even if I couldn't recognize a single one. I really wanted to find something like the wild mushrooms I used to bring my mother.

Early one morning, after we'd walked almost all night, we settled on a camping spot and Jenia and I went off together to forage. Dakhoun would have come, too, but I insisted on her staying and resting. Since they'd looked at her, the King and Queen of the Dreamies, I'd been particularly anxious about her. The constant presence of the little dark man didn't help.

When I came back with my arms full of wild onions and asparagus—there's a way you can cook them together—Dakhoun wouldn't wake up.

She was just lying there on her blanket, turned halfway on her side, very peacefully. Her head was resting on her open right hand. I still remember that, the same way I remember how I kept trying to call her by that other name.

I don't know how long I sat there in the drying dawn grass with Dakhoun's head in my lap. The sun didn't move; the sweet, meaningless weather kept going along, and the swooping, soaring, diving birds overhead were real birds now, even if I didn't recognize a one of them. There were more dandelions popping up all around than there had been the day before.

And the little dark man was sitting by her, looking as much at peace as she did.

Dakhoun seemed to be taking longer between each long, long breath, but that could have been just me breathing with her. What bothered me more than her breathing—at least it was regular and steady enough right now—was the changing that I couldn't pretend not to see, not to watch happening to her, in her.

She still looked like herself, like nobody else in the world: like the strange comforting shadow that had bent over me in the night at the end of the world, to wash me as clean as she could of what had become of me. But the stone was beginning to show through.

I put my hand on her cheek, on her throat, feeling the slow breath on my fingers and the distant whisper of her heart. The little dark man sat off by himself, seemingly unconcerned by any of this, as though whatever battle there had been between them was long over with. Twice I saw her closed eyelids tremble, and I spoke her name both times, but she never responded. There was no place now where I couldn't feel the otherness just beneath her skin, whether or not I could actually see the stony skeleton rising. I didn't know what to do for her. I could only keep whispering, like her heart.

I didn't look up until Jenia sat down next to me. I hardly recognized her; she appeared in that moment as far away as she had on my seventeenth birthday when I had my first vision of her, in the shadow of a high gray boulder. She looked across that space, questioning with her eyes. I shook my head, and we sat silently for a while, watching Dakhoun breathe. I kept smoothing her hair back, because the breeze kept disarranging it.

At last Jenia said, "All right. All right." She rose abruptly, nodding to me, so I stood, too. Jenia said,

"Father's song, that one he always used to sing to me. Do you remember that one?"

For answer I sang the first lines of the song: "'Up a tree and down a hill . . . apple butter, apple spill . . . ' I couldn't believe it when you sang it the other day."

"I don't remember much else," Jenia said quietly. "That song . . . maybe one or two others, I'm not sure." She hesitated, thinking seriously. "Oh, there was a story—I do remember the story. A little girl and a lion . . . and there was a fox, too, a fox who saved the little girl . . . ?"

I felt an odd twinge that shamed me for feeling it. That was *my* story, my special favorite, and he had told it to my sister—who wasn't my sister, who could never be my sister—before I was even born. But all I said was, "Yes, I know that story. Only it's a cat, a black cat. The way he told it. A wise black cat and a little girl."

"Oh. Yes, of course. Yes. A black cat."

We were quiet, while I kept my eyes on Dakhoun's face. Jenia kept watching me—I could see that out of the corner of my eye. Dakhoun's breath sounded peaceful and faraway, and I couldn't say why it frightened me so badly. I just kept trying to say her whole strange name, never getting it quite right.

"All right, then." Jenia whispered it this time. She turned sharply away from me, facing a thickly wooded hillside where I'd seen a hunting pair of foxes that morning, and she began again, singing:

> *Up a tree and down a hill,*
> *apple butter, apple spill,*
> *swing three times around the oak,*
> *morning music, midnight joke . . .*

Her voice grew stronger as she went on, and it seemed to me that the tree branches began to rustle just the smallest bit. And the little dark man, who'd looked to be almost dozing in the grass near Dakhoun, suddenly sat up to stare at the three of us: first at her, then briefly at me . . . and after that mostly at Jenia, who was standing up straight herself, with her head back and her voice and the wind somehow becoming the same thing, singing with all her full heart:

> *Up a tree and down a hill,*
> *apple butter, apple spill,*
> *swing three times around the oak,*
> *morning music, midnight joke . . .*

And the branches of those trees did begin to shake more and more violently, one and then the next, and then all, and the leaves were beating against each other as though something large and loud lived up there. And because I hadn't been paying attention to anything in the world but Dakhoun's slow, slowing breath, that's the first time I noticed that all the trees on that hillside were oaks.

Jenia never turned back toward us, not even to glance briefly at me. She simply started off, to walk around the biggest oak tree, taking her time, deliberately taking more time than you'd think she'd need, for all the size of that trunk. On the far side, she actually vanished for a few moments—again, just a bit longer than you might expect—and as she came back into view, her face was older than it had been when she disappeared. The little dark man watched every step she took finishing her first circuit of the oak tree. It took her a long time.

The second time around, she almost didn't make it. She was lurching and staggering, and I could hear her gasping all the long way . . . but somehow she kept going. Just as she reached us her legs went out from under her, and I only partway broke her fall as she collapsed beside me. She couldn't speak at all; all her strength went into breathing, and I didn't know what to do except to rub her shoulders. The oak leaves were blowing hard and angry now; the little dark man was already on his feet, his broken-leaf face definitely irritated. Dakhoun's eyelids were trembling, trying to open.

It felt like an age had passed before Jenia could finally

speak. Her voice was clear enough, but so shaky that I had to listen closely because the branches were whipping so. "I'm sorry. . . . I am so sorry. . . ."

"What are you talking about?" I demanded. "You did the best you could with a nursery rhyme—what did you expect? What was the whole point, anyway?"

Jenia was still catching her breath and shaking her head. "No, no, it was my fault. I knew what needed to be done, but I couldn't—I wasn't strong enough, I thought I could be, I was sure. . . . Oh, *Sooz* . . . !"

Now she was crying, crying exactly the way my father does, in absolute silence, eyes dry and body shaking like those oak branches on the windless hillside. I put my arms around her, awkward as ever, trying to grieve her grief without any idea of what it was. Someway, it was a little like Dakhoun holding me.

Jenia finally managed to say, "Sooz, you must understand, there is no other way home for you." I felt my face go completely, utterly cold, and she must have seen it, too, because she added quickly, "I mean for all of us, for you and her—Dakhoun—and for me as well. The king cannot command us back across their border, even if he wanted to, but he can keep us lost here in this . . . this *between* land as long as he pleases." She took a long, harsh breath before she went on. "This is about me, no one else. I am the one who offended him."

I stared at her. Jenia said, "The king and the queen

have no children. In all their land—and it is almost as endless as you imagine it—have you ever seen one single child yourself?" She sounded curious, as though she really wanted to know.

I said, "I'm not sure. Age is all scrambled here." Jenia smiled tightly, nodding for me to go on. "I mean, I've seen some who look so much younger than I am, but I know they're not—and then there are others who could be your age, or maybe a little older, but I can't tell." I was talking, but speech was coming slower than I meant it to. "If I think about it, I can't even tell anymore how long I've really been in this place."

Jenia's eyes still held mine, trying to make me see something I knew I didn't want to. I would have closed my own eyes if I could have.

Jenia said flatly, "The children they steal from mortals don't survive. No one knows why, not even the king, but they never do. Some live longer than others—I knew a boy who had come away with them well before me. That's what they call it, you know, *coming away*. . . . But he died, too, as they do. Always, always, Sooz."

"But not you!" I wasn't quite raising my voice, but it was a close thing. "You were going to be the special one! They promised you'd be living forever, like one of them! They said so!" It doesn't make any sense, but I found myself being indignant on my sister's behalf, even though she wasn't my sister. "They promised, you told me . . . and yet you decided—you chose to come home with us, just the same! I don't—"

I'll always be grateful that she interrupted me when she did. Jenia smiled at me, and I know past any doubt that whatever I am . . . whatever I really am . . . nobody ever smiled at me that completely. Not my parents, not even Molly Grue or King Lír . . . only Jenia, who was far, far less family than my Malka was to me. Only Jenia smiled at me so . . . Jenia and my stone friend, who was dying at my feet, and who never had been very much for smiling.

Jenia's face was as serenely resolved as her voice was trembling and afraid. She said, "Where should I die, but at home? Even if I don't remember home very well—nor my mother and father, not you at all, dear Sooz—where else should it be?" She laughed shakily, spreading her hands as she looked at me. "And *you* . . . you were so stubborn, so downright rock headed, you paid no attention to anything, not even me—you just kept *coming*, coming to find me, wherever I was hiding. . . ."

It's just as well that I was only partly listening, because I'm sure I'd have slipped like *that* into my old way of feeling like the idiot of the world; that's still too easy for me, even now. But what I was really paying attention to was the fact that neither of us singing my father's little nonsense bedtime song had changed anything. The oak leaves were still as busy as though *something* was just about to happen, but nothing was happening at all.

SOOZ

Up a tree and down a hill,
apple butter, apple spill . . .

Well, the first line could mean directions, someway—
but that second line I definitely knew about. That was his
old joke about the time my mother had spent all afternoon
preparing butter from our last apples of the season, and
he'd been hurrying through the kitchen and managed to
knock it off the fire and absolutely ruin it. It had become
one of those family stories everyone remembers forever,
even though I wasn't born then, and in time it ended as
part of that bedtime rhyme of his.

Swing three times around the oak . . .

Everyone knows oaks are magic, I've said that. It had
taken all Jenia's strength to walk all the way even once
around the biggest one on that hillside. That hadn't made
a bit of difference then, but what if the difference were
simply in that single word, *swing.* . . .

"Swing." I heard myself say it aloud. "Jenia. You *walked*
around the tree. But the song says *swing.* What if you just
didn't go around it fast enough?"

I remember her face, her standing and staring at me,
blinking in bewilderment. "But it's just a nursery song!
And the last line—*midnight music, midnight joke?* That's
the silliest part of all!"

205

"Only if you're just reaching for a rhyme. People do that all the time, just trying to find anything that fits." I'd made up little raggedy bits of songs myself, but I wasn't about to tell her about those. What I did do was to grab her by both shoulders and shake her to tell her what I suddenly knew beyond words all the way down inside. "A nursery rhyme isn't ever a silly song at all. Sometimes it can be a charm, a map to lead us home. But it won't work if we don't follow all the instructions exactly." I was breathing so hard that it was almost impossible to get the words out clearly. "Listen, Jenia, this is really, really important. You need to go around that oak three times—not just twice, you know that—and you need to *swing* around those trees, in a sort of way. . . ."

I tried to show her as well as I could, while she went on staring at me, just beginning to nod her head. I said, "Jenia, I never know when I'm right about anything, but this time I do know. This one time, I'm sure!"

But it wasn't possible. I knew that while the words were still coming out of my mouth. She couldn't yet stand up properly, let alone chance those oaks, as angry as they were. I was afraid of what might be waiting on the far side under the leaves, and I was afraid of leaving Dakhoun alone with that little dark man waiting on her last breath. And more than anything I was afraid of her opening her eyes at last to find me gone. But there wasn't any choice, if I wanted to get us all home. As it turned out, there never had been a choice.

I bent close to her face, so the little dark man wouldn't hear. "I have to go, I have to fix something, but it won't take long. You wait for me—I'll be back quickly." There was something more I wanted to say, but I didn't know how. "Don't you go anywhere without me." And I stood up.

The little dark man tried to bar my way, but I simply walked around him as though he were just another tree. He didn't block me any further, though he did say something I never bothered to hear. I had no concern with him. I took one long breath, murmured something myself, and started running.

No, that's not right, and it's hard to explain. I don't know what told me, but somehow I understood that *swinging* around the oak didn't exactly mean running. *Swinging* is something sort of somewhere between actual running and a really brisk walk, and it has much more to do with rhythm than speed. You have to feel it in your body, in your hips and knees, and you can't ever learn it, no one can teach you. I think when I started around that oak tree I was remembering the way Dakhoun had of moving, but that didn't feel right, either. I just braced myself lightly, briefly, against that oak tree, and I swung.

The first time around was easy enough. The leaves did keep brushing against my face, but nothing else seemed interested in delaying me. And I had a smooth, comfortable rhythm working, easing me as I touched that huge trunk, almost—but not quite—bouncing off it each time, and kept going. I can't describe it any better than that, but for once in my life I knew what I was doing. For once in my life I was altogether sure of . . . me.

But the second time . . .

Even knowing what Jenia had gone through during her one circuit of the tree, there was no possible way I could have prepared for what was waiting. If I hadn't kept on swinging around the trunk, brushing it quickly with my knuckles every time, I don't think I'd have done even as well as Jenia. It wasn't the leaves battering my face hard and steadily enough to bruise, it wasn't simply the half-buried acorns I stumbled over, nor the roots—the gnarly, twisty roots that hadn't been there before—now arching up hungrily to catch my feet so that I was constantly falling off my rhythm. . . . It was the *voices*, those voices I couldn't quite make out, whispering in the leaves all around my head, chattering and baying, so greedy, so eager, all I could do was struggle not to hear them. I feared first that it might be the evil little red-capped creatures that can infest the very oldest oaks; my father used to tell me about those. But these voices were different, wicked in a different way. . . .

You have to keep going—if you stop even a minute to catch your breath, it's all over. I can't say how I know this, I just do.

I managed one glance toward Dakhoun and Jenia as I wheezed into my third turn around the oak tree. The wild leaves were making it impossible for me to catch more than a single glimpse of the pair of them for an instant, Dakhoun just beginning to sit up, and Jenia bending to brace her with an arm around her shoulders. Then all that was gone, everything was gone, and there were only the voices and the wind. Or maybe the voices *were* the wind, and all that gale pushing back against every step, forcing me off my feet, the twigs and branches snapping and hungering, *but I mustn't fall down, mustn't, mustn't, mustn't*, all of it was me, my own stupidity, telling me every stupid thing I've ever done in my life from almost drowning Malka when I just knew I could swim in that stream and she had to save me, to running away from my father straight to those men those four men I have to not think about, when there was no Malka to save me, *mustn't, mustn't fall* because I'm just a dog anyway, just a basket dog like her, *the wind, mustn't, if I fall I'm done*, every stupid thing *every stupid stupid me*, poor stone Dakhoun just looking for Death and stranded forever with *stupid stupid me* . . .

And all the wind was gone, and of course I fell down flat and banged my nose really hard, and when I finally sat up, I was home.

We were home.

XII

THE LITTLE DARK MAN WASN'T A BIT HAPPY.

He was riding Dakhoun's shoulders as he always did, and he was still muttering and whispering in her ear, but she wasn't paying even the attention she'd have paid to a bug. Yes, she was veering off the path just maybe a now-and-then little, but she didn't stagger, nothing like that. Her head was high, and her pale eyes were clear, and I was right beside her, close as I could be without crowding. Jenia was walking along on her other side, silently there, just in case. Dakhoun was coming home with us, as she'd promised she would.

Death would have had trouble making himself heard anyway, because I was chattering to her like the most hysterical Dreamie you ever saw. "Look, Dakhoun, *look*—there's the tree where the fox family used to lair every winter! And *oh, there's* where we had that big fire I told you about, when we almost lost the house . . . and those big rocks, that's where Wilfrid used to dare me to climb to the top, and I beat him one time, only I broke my leg. . . ." Everything was all there, the way I remembered everything, and I couldn't stop because Dakhoun had to know all of it together, all of it all at once. "And over there, that's where we had the great mud-pie battle with the blacksmith's boys when they came down to visit their cousins, and Mother was so angry with me . . . and if you can see way, *way* over there—that shadow, that's the Midwood, where the griffin was. . . ." Chattering away, exactly like a Dreamie.

But even so, I did keep sneaking sidelong glances at Jenia, because even if she wasn't my sister, she was the real daughter of the house, after all, and yet she'd lost almost all of the childhood I knew, and I couldn't help from feeling sad and guilty about it, as though I'd somehow stolen it all from her. Which doesn't make sense to me, but what does anymore? She was gazing in every direction at everything—the whole field of spring lambs I hadn't met, either; the weary-looking rooks raising one more noisy new nest; the hill meadow where we drove the sheep to pasture every winter, except that very bad one when the wolves came down from the north. And I did want to tell her about my home—our home—just the same way I was busy telling Dakhoun, except Dakhoun didn't have time to learn it all. So I was hurrying—of course, I was hurrying. Of course, I was.

In these very last days, she'd come to look purely, finally herself. Almost all the human guise had simply slipped from her by now: not like a snake shedding its skin, but more like an animal changing altogether during its winter sleep and emerging as a completely different animal come spring. Like a butterfly. Like my friend. My Dakhoun.

Those eyes were the same as ever, seeing what they saw and not saying much about it. Beyond that . . . beyond that, all right, if you didn't know her, there's not a chance you'd have recognized her as anything but what she was. That old ragged peasant smock she still wore made it silly and almost clownish in a way, because she was so much more beautiful in her stone skin than anyone I'd ever seen in my life, or ever will see again.

She moved like summer water in the sun, and she knew where she was going, and she was exactly where she should be, there beside me. When I reached out for her hand, the old rough sorrow of her fingers rasped mine, and I held on with all the strength I had.

And she died even so. She turned to me with just a bit of a surprised look on her lovely, lovely stone face, and she said, "*There* . . . I told you I would bring you home, Sooz." And it was, and she had, and my mother and father were coming, and what a small house it really was when you see it after all this time, and they were both running and stumbling, and Dakhoun whispered, "You go home now, Sooz," and she let go of my hand.

She was so heavy at the last. When she fell, the sound shook the world.

I don't think anyone noticed the little dark man when he stood up over the body. He didn't keep me from closing her eyes, and he didn't make that mocking face of his, when I stroked her face and awkwardly kissed her forehead. And when she rose herself, when she rose in her magic spirit so quietly, no one else but me ever noticed that at all. Well, *he* did, of course, but he did wait for me.

There's a lot I missed, as there always is, because I was blinking so much. I remember my father holding Jenia as though she might die, too, at any moment, and my mother kneeling over Dakhoun's body with me, crying terribly herself out of such grief and such raw thanks. It was only then that she turned to me and looked long into my face. I don't recall anything she said, except, "I don't care what you are, you're mine. Do you hear me?"

Then she put her arms around me. I looked over her shoulder and I saw the little dark man ever so far down the road, and Dakhoun with him, still looking back. And I reached toward her and I told her what I told her . . . and then those strange other words came to me from somewhere, somewhere, "*Sunlight on your road.* . . ." I said that, too, and she smiled at me, she did. . . .

Then they were gone together, but for just another moment I know I saw the Queen of the Dreamies, alone by herself on that same road, staring out of those strange lost eyes toward Jenia, who never saw her because my father was holding her so tightly. Then she was gone, too, they were all gone, and in time we all went home together.

But I told Jenia about the Queen of the Dreamies that night, because that's the thing that matters. Because you can't forget the ones who change you always, the ones who won't ever forget you even if you should pass yourself and forget them. Who claim you forever. Whatever they are, wherever they are, whoever. Oh, whoever.

ACKNOWLEDGMENTS

I have a reasonable number of perfectly acceptable buddies, but very few lifelong friends. Friends, as I know them, are the ones you call at two in the morning when you need to know right now that at least somebody knows exactly who you are, and loves you anyway. This short list includes . . .

KATHLEEN HUNT, who is my lawyer, my dear treasured friend, and my stalwart, eternally comforting bulwark against my equally eternal midnight dread that whatever it is I do, I can't remember how I used to do it. . . .

DEBORAH GRABIEN, who has been, and continues to be, aggravatingly right about the right word, phrase, description, plot twitch, or character being precisely in the exactly right place, even when I wish she weren't. . . .

ACKNOWLEDGMENTS

JESSICA WADE, my editor on *The Way Home*, who is far too young to be as wise as she is. . . .

And HOWARD MORHAIM, who is my literary agent, and a late-blooming wonder of my late old age. Howard, to my wonder and marvel, actually gets things done and astonishing deals made. If he turns out actually to have made a deal with Satan, I will simply have to buy him out of it. I'd trust him to do the same for me.

Author photograph by Kathleen Hunt

PETER S. BEAGLE was born in 1939 and raised in the Bronx, just a few blocks from Woodlawn Cemetery, the inspiration for his first novel, *A Fine and Private Place*. Today, thanks to classic works such as *The Last Unicorn*, *Tamsin*, and *The Innkeeper's Song*, he is acknowledged as America's greatest living fantasy author, and his dazzling abilities with language, characters, and magical storytelling have earned him many millions of fans around the world.

Peter has written numerous teleplays and screenplays in addition to his stories and novels. They include the animated versions of *The Lord of the Rings* and *The Last Unicorn*, plus the fan favorite "Sarek" episode of *Star Trek: The Next Generation*. His nonfiction book, *I See by My Outfit*, which recounts a 1963 journey across America on motor scooter, is considered a classic of American travel writing. He is also a gifted poet, lyricist, and singer/songwriter.

VISIT PETER S. BEAGLE ONLINE

Beagleverse.com

PeterSBeagleBooks

Beagleverse_Official

Ready to find
your next great read?

Let us help.

Visit prh.com/nextread

Penguin
Random
House